Nice Kitty?

"Hey, Hobie, look, it's our old friend,"
Nick shouted, pointing ahead at the side of
the road. "Here, kitty, kitty," he called,
running ahead. "Here, owl!" The creature
moved toward us slowly as we galloped his
way, calling and whistling. And I bet we
were only ten feet away before I saw that,
while he *was* black and white, he wasn't our
cat. This kitty was big and black and furry
with white stripes down both sides and had
eyes like tiny red marbles. He was a skunk!

Books by Jamie Gilson

CAN'T CATCH ME, I'M THE GINGERBREAD MAN
DIAL LEROI RUPERT, DJ
DO BANANAS CHEW GUM?
4B GOES WILD
THIRTEEN WAYS TO SINK A SUB

Published by ARCHWAY paperbacks

4B Goes Wild

by Jamie Gilson

illustrated by
Linda Strauss Edwards

AN ARCHWAY PAPERBACK
Published by POCKET BOOKS • NEW YORK

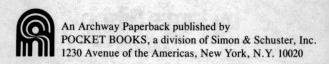
An Archway Paperback published by
POCKET BOOKS, a division of Simon & Schuster, Inc.
1230 Avenue of the Americas, New York, N.Y. 10020

Published by arrangement with Lothrop, Lee & Shepard Books,
a division of William Morrow & Company, Inc.
Library of Congress Catalog Card Number: 83-948

ISBN: 0-671-50984-5

First Archway Paperback printing September, 1984

10 9 8 7 6 5 4 3 2

AN ARCHWAY PAPERBACK and colophon are
trademarks of Simon & Schuster, Inc.

Cover design by Milton Charles

Printed in the U.S.A.

IL3+

For Matthew,
who knows how to call owls,
push cows,
and sanitize the telephone
for your protection

Contents

4B Goes Wild

Dinosaur Delight

"You know what Dinosaur Delight sounds like? It sounds like ice cream with salted fossils," I told Nick. "Just the *sound* hurts my teeth. I'd rather spend my Saturday cleaning the cat's box than going to a Dinosaur Delight."

Nick Rossi was walking his front porch rail, tilting like a stunt airplane. He tipped, flapping his arms, and almost crashed into the juniper bushes. I was next door in my yard filling my bike tires with fresh air after their long, flat winter. It had rained the night before, and worms lay on the sidewalk gagging for air.

"It was my *mother* who thought up that name!" Nick yelled. He jumped to the porch and whipped a fat green rubber frog at me. It sailed way over my head. I couldn't have reached it

1

with accordion arms. Toby, Nick's little brother, ran after it into my yard.

"Frogger!" he shrieked. "Mine!" Toby is four, and the frog *was* his.

"It's because my mom knew the fourth grades would be doing dinosaurs now," Nick went on. "She said we'd go bananas over a fair called Dinosaur Delight. So that just shows how much *you* know, Hobie Hanson."

"I know we studied almost an hour for the dumb test yesterday, and I know that's enough dinosaurs for me." I lifted the frog from Toby's clutch. "Besides, I'm going to ride my bike today all the way down the Green Bay trail."

Toby stomped on my foot. I dropped the frog on his head. Nick and Toby's mother is big in the Central School PTA. She's head of something called Ways and Means. That's a bunch of people, Nick says, who figure out ways to make money. The Dinosaur Delight was one of those ways.

Actually, every spring the PTA throws a fair in the gym. Last year it was the Jungle Jamboree. My dad took me and wanted to leave after five minutes. The place was decorated with tons of crepe paper and pink-and-yellow snakes that curled down through the basketball nets. My dad couldn't believe it. Pink-and-yellow snakes! People sold cookies and other stuff they'd made. But the worst part was a bunch of third and fourth grade girls dressed up like leopards who hopped around selling alligator whistles and chocolate-covered animal crackers. They made jungle-type noises, held their hands up like paws, and thought they were incredibly cute. My dad said we should leave before he stepped on one.

"I won't go," I said, pumping away on my back tire. One more squirt of air, I thought, the tire will be full and I'll be free. "Dinosaurs are extinct and I'm glad."

Toby sat on the grass at my feet and ground dandelion heads on his knees, covering them with bright yellow dots. Then he reached over and twisted a splotch on the toe of my grungy gym shoe. "Hey, Hobie, you know what?" he called up to me. "You like butter, too!"

"Hobie Hanson!" Mom called out the living room window. "Are you and your father going to that Dinosaur Delight thing with Nick or not?"

"Come on," Nick grumbled. "I'm not going to that thing by myself."

"Not!" My dad called from the garden out back. "I've got a glitch in my side from too much digging."

"Not!" I told her, and Nick spun around and banged toward his front door.

"Great," she said. "Then you can help me take down the storm windows. I'll just send the money to school with Nick."

"Do I have to?" I groaned.

Nick grinned and jumped down the steps. "You can't win, Hanson. When do we leave?"

"Oh, Hobie, you know what else?" Mom said, sticking her head out again.

"Yeah, I know. I haven't changed Fido's litter."

"Right."

The early April sun was warm, but the air still smelled like it had just rained. Even on a good day, Fido's litter box does not smell like fresh rain. I had been pumping my back tire for about five minutes, and it was still your basic flat back tire. Something was wrong. If I'd pumped that much air into a kickball, it would have exploded.

"And your father needs some help in . . ." Mom started.

"I know. I know." Dinosaurs were beginning to sound like prime-time TV. Maybe the fair would be fabulous and not cutesie. Maybe none of the fourth grade girls would be wearing weird costumes and selling things.

"I've changed my mind," I told her, and she smiled. "I'll do all that stuff when I get back. Nick would probably lose the money anyway."

Nick flicked a black spider at me by the long rubber band in its back. Toby yanked out a handful of grass and started to sweep the sidewalk clear of beached worms.

Handing me a ten-dollar bill, Mom said that if they weren't gone I was to buy a dozen of Mrs. Bosco's famous chewy walnut brownies that she made for every bake sale and to spend the rest the way I wanted to because it was for such a good cause. Then she went back to exchanging storm windows for screens.

After I'd stashed my sick bike in the garage, Nick and I started out for school. It seemed weird on a Saturday morning. Especially at nine-thirty. We knew there wasn't going to be a bell at the other end. Or a kickball game before the bell. Or Mr. Star with a spelling test.

"Hold up," Toby yelled. We turned and watched him scramble to his feet.

"You're not going with us," I called to him. "This is for the big kids." He stuck out his bottom lip and sucked in enough breath for a major shriek.

"Oh, didn't I tell you?" Nick said, inspecting his gym shoes. "We're taking Toby." He went on fast. "Mom had to be there at seven-thirty this morning to set up."

Toby can be a pain. He's got a whine like fingernails scraping a chalkboard. But there didn't seem to be any way out. The cat's box in the basement was still full, my father still needed help planting asparagus, and the winter windows were still up. Toby's not *that* much of a pain. So we started off, Nick and I walking, Toby riding his Kermit the Frog Big Wheel with Kermit peering over his shoulder from the backrest.

"What's this 'good cause,'" I asked Nick, "that my mom gave me ten dollars to spend on? She has *never* given me ten dollars, not even to buy my grandmother a birthday present."

"School stuff," Nick said, shrugging. "You know, like last year when the fifth graders got on buses and went to hear the symphony—the PTA paid."

"Very educational." I yawned. "That sounds like something my mother would think was worth ten dollars."

"You know what we get this year?"

"We learn how to rotate crops."

"Close."

"Oral hygiene lessons?"

"Right!"

"You're kidding."

"Right." He grinned at me. "This year we go on an overnight."

"Come on."

"And put a whole *school* of fish between Miss Hutter's sheets."

"Outdoor Ed!" I yelled. "They're letting us go? I thought after last year they were never going to have Outdoor Ed again. Hiding a catfish in the principal's bed was too much. That's what they said."

Nick started walking backward in front of me. "They lied."

"The whole fourth grade? Our class *and* Ms. O'Malley's?" I asked him. "All night long?"

"Two nights," he said, "at this camp almost ninety miles away in Wisconsin. Mom says we'll be in a big lodge place—the boys *and* the girls. And the teachers, too, I guess. Mom says they've

6

decided we're more *mature* than last year's fourth graders."

I rolled my eyes at him. I'd been mad when I thought we weren't going, but now I wasn't so sure. I'd never been away from home in another state—not without my folks. A couple of sleepovers, sure, but . . .

"Besides," he went on, "they're sending in more chaperones. There'll be Miss Hutter and Mr. Star and Ms. O'Malley, and anybody else they can con into it, I guess."

"Hold up!" Toby called from half a block back. We held up.

He was frowning as he pedaled toward us. "My pants are wet," he said.

"That's because you've been sitting in the grass and it rained last night," I told him.

"Really?" he asked. He frowned again and turned his Big Wheel around. "I want to go home."

"You'll dry," I told him.

"You can't be homesick," Nick explained, "we're not that far from home. Besides, Mom is at school and she needs you there holding onto her leg while she walks around the gym." We kept going.

Toby sat still for a minute, deciding. Then he honked the frog-croaking horn, leaned back, and cranked like crazy to catch up with us. *"Zoom,"* he zoomed, and sped between us to wait at the corner.

When we finally got to school, Nick opened the front door and let Toby steam down the hall like it was the Indy 500. If they caught him inside on his Big Wheel, he'd wail and they'd let him off just for the quiet. If they caught me inside on my bike, I'd get life for sure with no time off for good behavior. Toby left his wheels at the gym door like a big deal who doesn't care beans if he gets a ticket.

But when we stepped inside, he turned into a little kid again. He didn't bound off and grab his mother's leg like Nick said he would. He picked mine instead and hugged it like he was trying to squeeze toothpaste out the top. It's true that the sweaty old gym looked wild. From the ceiling hung the huge white silk parachute we sometimes use in gym class. It was strung from all four basketball hoops and it sagged low, like a cloud about to pour. Each of the hoops was covered by a nest of fuzzy brown-paper strips with a ptero-dactyl plopped on top. While marching from class to gym the week before we'd peered through the art room door to see the sixth graders make those pterodactyls out of papier maché. The bodies were purple, the batlike wings drooped, and the orange beaks opened wide, like they were ready to snap up a bellyful of little kid. Toby peeked at them from behind my knee.

"Hey, Tobe, we'll see you later," Nick yelled over his shoulder, charging through clumps of parents and kids. When I tried to follow him, I had to walk like Frankenstein, dragging my Toby leg as I went.

And just as I was about to give him a fast shake, I went blind. *Zap,* just like that. These hands gripped my eyes from behind and a girl's voice said, very high, "I am a dinosaur. If you guess who I am you get a free gift."

"I don't want a free gift." I tried to pull loose, but my anchor held fast. Toby was sitting on my foot, his legs wrapped around my leg. And his pants *were* wet. I hoped it really was because he'd been sitting in the damp grass.

"Clue number one," the voice said. "I have jaws like a crocodile and teeth like daggers."

"You're Molly Bosco," I answered, because that's who was holding my eyes.

"Dwerp," she said, and squeezed tighter. I saw flashy yellow stars like Fourth of July sparklers. "You've got to try or it isn't any fun."

Toby grabbed my hand.

"Clue number two," the high voice charged on. "I have fierce claws and I am the Brontosaurus's biggest enemy. I hold down my prey and tear the flesh off his bones."

"Sounds more like a Mollybosco all the time."

"She's an Allosaurus," Toby said from the floor. He'd learned that when Nick and I studied for the test. It was his favorite dinosaur by far. "Al-lo-saur-us," he said like he was licking a lollipop. He unwrapped himself from my foot. My sock was damp.

9

"Double dwerp," Molly muttered, and let go of my eyes. Toby wandered off toward a game called Tar Pits where his mother was selling tickets. I turned to see Molly's cute little Allosaurus costume, but she wasn't wearing one. She had on jeans and a sweater dotted with red hearts. Her dark brown hair bounced as she and Lisa Soloman flapped their arms, waving the helium balloons tied to their wrists.

"Great costume," I told her. "Especially the jaws, claws, and teeth like daggers."

Molly did not smile.

Lisa laughed until she saw Molly looking grim. "Nobody wanted to make costumes this year," she told me.

Molly shrugged. "My grandmother says dinosaurs are extinct because their shapes don't make sense. She sewed a whole batch of Stegosaurus capes, though, for the Tar Pits game."

"You want a balloon?" Lisa asked, holding her wrist out to me.

"I didn't win it."

"You knew, though. We just had a test."

"No answer, no prize," Molly said, pushing Lisa aside. "Hobie, you better go buy your door-prize tickets. They're going to draw the winners at—" Suddenly she stopped talking, put her finger to her lips, and pointed to the gym door. Her balloons flipped through the air.

Lisa turned and tiptoed around behind Marshall Ezry, who stood facing the other end of the gym. She snuck up on him, flung her hands over his eyes, and began her memorized speech. "I am a dinosaur. If you guess who I am you get a free gift. Clue number one: I-am-the-biggest-and-heaviest-of-the-dinosaurs."

"If-you-do-not-let-my-eyes-go-I-will-flip-you-and-you-will-be-the-*flattest*-of-dinosaurs," Marshall said, very calm. "You will be a dinosaur *rug*."

I decided Marshall could take care of himself, so I wandered around to see what I could spend Mom's ten dollars on. At the first long table somebody was painting names on barrettes. The next one had kids' high school brothers and sisters drawing hearts and flowers and skulls on people's cheeks and foreheads. Then there was a booth with silver star wands and little tinsel crowns, not high on the list of stuff I wanted.

Mrs. Bosco, Molly's huge, half-deaf grandmother, was in charge of the bake sale table. And across the gym I could see Nick with R.X. Shea and Rolf Pfutzenreuter. They were trying to win goldfish in little plastic Baggies. It didn't seem very dinosaur to me, but I was about to go win one myself as a pet for Fido when this hand with about four rings on it grabbed my shoulder. Mrs. Bosco had escaped from her booth.

"I have a batch of brownies for you, sonny," she boomed, guiding me over to the long table covered with plates of gingerbread men and chocolate chip cookies and carrot cake with white icing an inch thick. "My brownies always, *always* go first. And if your mother hadn't warned my daughter you were coming, I wouldn't have saved any. I've been telling people they're all sold."

I have to admit, her brownies *are* always fantastic. They are thick and rich and gooey like fudge, with chunks of walnuts in all the right places. Even piled on a paper plate covered with plastic wrap, their dark-chocolatey smell leaked out and curled into my mouth.

"I thought your father was coming. Where is he?" she shouted, snapping the ten-dollar bill from my hand.

"Home, I guess," I told her. She gave me eight dollars and a broken oatmeal-raisin cookie in change.

"Well, sonny, have your mother and father finally stopped fighting?" she yelled. People for yards around turned slightly to listen. I wondered how she got that. Then I remembered when my mom called Molly's about the brownies. She'd said how my dad is stubborn as a mule about going to the doctor for gas pains. And how when she wanted him to go he said he didn't need to pay forty dollars to find out he eats too many cucumbers. Molly's mom must have spread the word. Mrs. Bosco, though, made it sound like they were going at each other with bows and arrows.

"Pretty much," I said loud, so she could hear,

but that didn't sound quite right. "It's no big deal," I went on, but people had turned away. "I've gotta go," I mumbled through a mouthful of cookie and fled to the other side of the gym. Next she'd be asking if I didn't think Molly was the cutest girl in fourth grade.

Halfway across, Toby ran up and spun around to show me the cape he was wearing. "I won this in the Tar Pits," he said. "I got out. That's how you win." The cape was brown cloth with a hood that reached to his eyelashes. All the way from his forehead down his back was a mountain range of scales shaped like triangles.

"What do dinosaurs say?" he asked, scraping at my jeans with his claws and aiming for my wrist with his teeth.

"Roogie-roogie," I told him, holding my arms over my head.

"Roogie-roogie," he answered. "Can I have one of your brownies? They smell good."

"No, you can't. They're poison," I said, and kept walking.

"Last call for door-prize tickets," a crackly voice announced on the loudspeaker. "Fifty cents a ticket, two for a dollar. Eight big prizes: a luxury weekend for two at the Marriott, a weekday lunch at the Chuckwagon, Stockton's finest food, with Mr. Star, Mr. Vaccarella, or our very own principal, Miss Hutter, and more, much more. Get your razzle-dazzle, high-class prize tickets here."

Nick, R.X., and Rolf were still at the goldfish booth, each of them clutching a fat Baggie of goldfish and water.

"My dad did it when he was in college," Rolf was saying.

"You lie."

"I don't either. I think there's something about it in the *Guinness Book of World Records*."

"About your dad?"

"About people swallowing goldfish." He held

up his bag, and the fish fluttered in its tight, shiny pond. "My dad swallowed three of them *live*," he said, slowly opening the bag.

"That must feel weird in your stomach," R.X. said.

"But why would anybody want to?" I asked him. Then it occurred to me that *he* wanted to. "I bet you won't," I told him. *"I* wouldn't."

"I'm thinking about it," Rolf said, and stuck two fingers into the bag.

"Absolutely the last and final call for tickets," the crackly voice announced again.

"People eat sardines head and all," Rolf said. "I think."

"They're cooked first."

"In Japan they eat raw fish," Nick said. "I don't see why Rolf can't if he wants to."

"Not live, they don't," I told him. By then Rolf had his whole hand in the bag. My stomach felt like the goldfish was in it chasing the cornflakes I'd had for breakfast. So I hurried over to the woman at the microphone and gave her my eight dollars.

"All of it?" she asked.

"It's for the weekend at the Marriott," I told her. "My folks really need it." I thought about Dad planting the garden and Mom cleaning the house, getting everything ready for hot weather and stuff without me helping—they deserved a vacation.

"Oh, really?" she said, raising her eyebrows.

Then her voice turned all cotton candy sweet. "What *was* that I heard Mrs. Bosco say about their fighting?" She rested her hand on my shoulder. "Is it *very* serious?"

"No!" I told her, shaking her hand off. She raised her eyebrows.

While I signed my name on the stubs, she said to the woman next to her putting tickets into a big barrel, "That dear sweet Hanson child bought eight dollars' worth of tickets just so his parents could have a weekend together. Had you heard they were separating?"

"Wants to prevent the divorce," the other woman whispered to her. "Thinks it's all his fault. Sounds like a classic case of guilt to me."

I don't know why some people talk about kids like they're not there. "You've got it all wrong," I explained to them and they looked serious at each other and then smiled at me sweet, like I was a cute pink bunny rabbit.

"Oh, but don't you think it's a *dear* thing," the first woman said, looking straight at me, "for him to think of his parents instead of playing all of the games and eating all the lovely treats?"

"Geez, you did it," I heard Nick gasp. "I never thought you'd really do it."

When I turned around, Rolf was standing with an empty bag of water in his hand, his face pale green and a funny smile twitching on his lips.

"Can you feel its tail move?" R.X. asked in a quiet voice.

17

"Yeah," he said, his smile quivering. He started toward the gym door very slowly, then faster. Then he broke into a run and dropped the plastic bag *plotch* on the floor. Our gym teacher, Ms. Lucid, would banish him forever if she found out.

"All gather round for door prizes," the loudspeaker blared. Nick's mom had taken over. Toby was standing next to her on a chair, the barrel of tickets in front of him.

"I never win anything," R.X. said.

"You won the goldfish," Nick told him.

"Yeah, but that wasn't luck. That was skill. I'm a world-class ring tosser."

"You suppose Rolf made it to the john?"

"I doubt it."

"You think he'll tell his dad?"

"And the big luxury weekend, *including* a champagne brunch, goes to . . ."

Toby reached in, pulled out a ticket, and handed it to his mom. "Roogie-roogie," he said into the mike.

" . . . number four-five-one, that's four-five-one," Mrs. Rossi announced, breathless. "And the name on the back is . . . Ginny Massie. Oh, she's not able to be here, but I know she and Mel will have a fabulous time." People *oh*-ed and *ah*-ed.

The women who had sold me the tickets tisk-tisked my way, and the one who'd said I was a dear sweet thing shrugged her shoulders like "That's life, kid."

The next prizes a lot of kids wanted. A weekday lunch at the Chuckwagon three blocks away meant sitting on stools at the counter and ordering real hamburgers and fries while everybody at school was eating plastic lasagna. The first one was with Mr. Vaccarella, a really neat fifth grade teacher. Michelle Duguid in my class won that. I thought she was going to die giggling. Lunch with Mr. Star went to some kids' mother. Her kids were in kindergarten and second grade, so Mr. Star said if she would rather have an evening's free babysitting, he'd do that instead. The mother said, "Good grief, yes."

The other lunch taker was Miss Hutter. Miss Hutter doesn't look like she ever ate a hamburger in her life. She wears dresses with bows at the neck and little half glasses, and her idea of a costume on Halloween is a white sunbonnet. My parents like her because they say she is "no nonsense."

"And the winner of the lunch with Miss Hutter is . . ."

Toby drew out a long string of tickets that hadn't been separated.

" . . . somebody who bought a batch," Mrs. Rossi announced over the speaker, "somebody who must want to have lunch with our principal pretty badly . . ." She took the wad of tickets from Toby, beamed out at us all, and announced, "It's Hobie Hanson!"

"Roogie-roogie," Toby said.

I should have stayed at home and cleaned the cat's box.

On Trial

"GOOD morning, class," Mr. Star said, like he does every morning after the last bell.

"Good morning, Mr. Star," we answered all together, like we'd done every day since school began.

This time, after he'd checked the roll and cafeteria count and after we'd said the Pledge, Mr. Star leaned back against his desk and stared at us like he was trying to decide for sure if we were good apples or rotten.

"Well, 4B," he began, seriously, "it appears we're going to do it." It? We shot quick looks at each other and wondered. Run the mile? Skip recess forever? Teach old dogs new tricks?

"If everything goes well," he went on, "we

are, contrary to an earlier decision, going on Outdoor Education this year."

It was for sure, then. My ears began to prickle, and woollyworms to crawl around in my stomach. There was a ripple of "Wow" in the class. Yelps of joy.

"At a cost, I might add, of only eleven-fifty per person because of Saturday's highly successful Dinosaur Delight. What do you think of that?" He smiled like he thought it was fantastic.

"I'll tell him," I thought in a flash, "that I can't afford it."

"Scholarships, of course, are available," he went on, pacing up and down in front of the chalkboard. "Now, I expect you've all heard how a few of last year's fourth graders spoiled the trip for everyone with their childish, immature pranks. So, when Miss Hutter asked me some weeks ago if I thought room 4B was ready for a nature study trip, I had to think long and hard." He rubbed his head like all that thinking had pained him. "But I told her that 4B was ready. So, three weeks from today, if you've been perfect or near perfect in every way, we and room 4A—the whole fourth grade—will spend three days at Camp Trotter in Wisconsin."

Three days meant two nights. Two nights away from home. In another state. My heart was chuffing like I'd dashed down the hall to beat the bell, and my head swarmed with ways to be a whole lot less than perfect so they'd call the whole thing

22

off. But I kept smiling like I thought it was great. Some flags you don't wave.

"Now, I have a packet of information for each of you to take home to your parents or guardians this afternoon explaining what we plan to do in Outdoor Education Studies and what you need to bring. I don't want any of them stuck in your lockers and forgotten."

It wouldn't do any good to leave the stuff in my locker. Parents have a way of hearing about things like that. But I *could* plan to have a stomachache.

"My grandmother has volunteered to come as a chaperone, what with so many mothers working," Molly chirped, like she not only *knew* already about the trip, but knew *all* about it.

"The first thing we're going to do in preparation," Mr. Star said, as he erased Friday's assignments from the board, "is to change gears in science. Now that we've finished the unit on dinosaurs, this afternoon we'll be moving on to the live animals of our woods—including skunks."

Everybody laughed. Skunks sound funny.

Nick raised his hand. "Hey, we're going from *ex*-tinct to stinked," he said, and everybody laughed.

Mr. Star lowered his head and looked grim. "That, Nicholas, was uncalled for." And then he smiled. "You stole my punch line. I should fine you a dollar for theft." Nick groaned, reached in his desk, and pulled out a bill of Monopoly money, but Mr. Star waved it away, laughing.

"In any case, it's court time," Mr. Star went on. For two whole months we'd been studying local government, and our room was set up like a town. We named it Stardom, short for Mr. Star's kingdom, though, of course, it was *supposed* to be a democracy. Anyway, most of our desks were pushed back against the walls of the room, and each of us had masking-tape markers on the floor to show the land we owned around our desks. It was our private property. The places that weren't marked off private were streets and parks, except for Mr. Star's desk in the corner. That was City Hall, and he was the big shot.

Molly's desk was against the windows next to City Hall, then me, then Jenny Hanna and Tracey Hogrefe and Eugene Kim and Aretha Eliott. Mr. Star had tried to boy-girl-boy-girl us, but there were too many girls to make it come out right. Nick sat across the room next to Michelle and then Marshall. Rolf was one of the kids whose desks were clumped together as apartment buildings in the big middle space we called Central Park.

Also in Central Park was the courthouse. It was a round yellow table, actually, and when we had court, we put a chair on the table for the person accused of the crime. We had city council meetings and park board meetings, and we set up businesses and stuff, but we all liked court best.

Somebody was always suing somebody for something—five dollars and up for bugging, ten dollars for tripping. There was a whole list of possibilities.

"Fifteen minutes for court today, no more. That's all we can spare," Mr. Star announced.

"But we've got seventeen cases," Molly said. "That's no fair."

"Most courts have too many cases. Fifteen minutes."

"OK, court-is-in-session-order-in-the-court," Lisa said, fast as firecrackers. She was bailiff. Molly, who was judge, sat down on the orange judge's stool. "The first case is Michelle versus Hobie." She banged the gavel on the edge of the table. "Hurry up, Hobie. We haven't got forever."

I climbed onto the table and sat in the chair looking out over the class like I was king of the mountain.

"Are you innocent or guilty?" Molly asked.

"Innocent," I told her. "I was framed."

"Guilty, guilty, guilty," Michelle sighed, shaking her head like she was sorry for me that I had to lie.

The rest of the class was listening only halfway. Most of them were whispering or passing notes about the sleepover camp. Mr. Star was working on some papers at his desk. Eugene had folded his arms on the back of his chair and was resting his head on them.

25

Molly shifted on the judge's stool. Around her waist she wore a belt that was printed MOLLY-MOLLYMOLLY. She had two barrettes from the fair that said MOLLYMOLLYMOLLY on them, too. Not that anybody was going to forget. I had my baseball cap on, backward.

"What are the charges?" she asked Michelle.

"The charges are that Hobie pushed me, your honor," Michelle said.

"The charge sheet says it was nine fifty-two in the morning," Lisa reported.

It had happened at nine fifty-two two weeks ago, so it hardly seemed worth fighting about. But Molly had forgotten to make me promise to tell the whole truth and nothing but the truth, so I lied.

"Your honor, I didn't do it," I said.

Michelle's face turned red and she banged her fist on the table my chair sat on, and it shook. She loved going to court. She played it like a TV soap. "Your honor, he did so! You did so push me!" she yelled. "You pushed me on Marshall's land and he's suing me for trespassing." Marshall grinned and tipped his baseball cap at us.

"All I know is, I didn't, or if I did, I didn't mean it."

"You have any witnesses?" Molly asked her.

She had four, all girls. And so I got fined two hundred dollars, the most you could be fined for pushing.

"I thought you might try to get out of it by using your *in*fluence," Rolf called as I handed over the money. "I mean, you're going to have lunch with the prin-ci-pal, aren't you? Wow-*ee!*" I could have poked him, but since I'd just gotten fined for pushing, it didn't seem right. Besides, the possibility of witnesses was pretty good. Also, the fine doubled the second time around, and my money supply was getting low.

Molly banged the gavel again. I stood up and stretched like I didn't care beans for losing two hundred dollars to Michelle and climbed down from the defendant's chair as slowly as possible.

"Next case," Molly declared and read off Jenny versus Aretha, who had other girls be lawyers for them.

"What did those guys do last year on Outdoor Ed that was so bad?" Eugene asked me as soon as I got back to my seat. "It must have been awful."

"Just stuff," I said. "Frogs in the girls' shower stalls and like that."

He leaned over to my ear. "Have you ever been far away from home at night?" he whispered.

"Lots of times," I lied. "We slept in tents and thought we heard bears in the night, and bats." I did do that once in Nick's backyard, but it rained, so we went home to bed before midnight. "How about you?"

"Oh, sure," he said, straightening up. "Sure. Lots of times. I'm not scared or anything. I was just wondering." And he started to laugh.

"Order in the court," Lisa called. "Any more disturbances and I'll clear the room."

After Aretha was found not guilty of stealing the top of Jenny's blue pen because half the class has blue pens just like it and who's to know whether the top on Aretha's desk was Jenny's or not, Mr. Star gave us a spelling test of local government words. I missed munisiple . . . munecipal . . . municipal.

But I was great at recess. I shine at recess. It was an excellent warm kickball recess day. And when that ball came at me fast and smooth at the end of our inning, I made a crater a mile deep in it with my toe. We had two on base—R.X. and Aretha. My ball sailed up, hit a cloud or two, and angled down into the spit pit, and that meant we were all home free. It also meant I would get two points for kicking a pit ball. That made the score four to three. I strolled, very casual, toward first base, a hero.

The spit pit is this disgusting staircase next to the playground that is filled with gross junk. Kids sometimes spit in it, and nobody likes to slip on all the mold getting kickballs out. So it was like somebody had waved a magic wand or something when, just as I was about to tap first base, the ball popped out of the pit. It sailed back up and onto the field like a movie playing in reverse.

Geez, I thought, there's a seal in there escaped from Lincoln Park Zoo. It's sliding down the spit pit steps, flipping balls off its nose. I didn't see how that ball could possibly have *bounced* out because the place is crammed with mud-crusted mittens and scarves, rotten bananas, and at least one three-page paper on the life and death of Tyrannosaurus Rex. Those things a ball would just sink its seams into.

But there it was, my pit ball back in play. I ran like crazy toward second. But, wouldn't you know, the ball was aimed straight *at* second. Michelle, who'd already won two hundred dollars from me in court, caught it and tagged me out. Just like that.

My team all started screaming and demanding a replay and calling foul and cheat. There was a lot of pushing and shoving, too, until Mr. Star raised his voice. "OK, friends. What did I say about good behavior? You keep this up and 4B will definitely *not* be along for Outdoor Ed. Think about it."

There was this silence while we all stared at the pebbly black asphalt and thought about it. If I tackled Michelle, would they keep us home? Probably not. Besides, somebody might figure out why I did it.

"How'd I do?" a low, old voice called from somewhere under ground level. "Didn't break anything, did I?"

We all turned again to the spit pit, but it wasn't

the seal from Lincoln Park Zoo whose fringed bald head we saw. It was Mr. Gosnell, the custodian. He was chuckling. "Boy, that thing shot at me like Halley's comet." He had a black plastic sack slung over his shoulder and a shovel in his hand.

We all stood staring. "Heading straight at my head, it was. So I stepped back, wound up, and . . ." He put the bag down, grabbed the shovel with two hands, and, using it like a bat, showed us how he'd slammed the ball out of the pit. He rolled his shoulders around like it had been *some* jolt, too. Then, picking the fat bag back up and heading toward the trashroom, he said, "I'm giving that stairwell a good spring cleaning. Lots of stuff blows down there during the wintertime, you know."

The bell rang. The game was over, and my team had lost. But nobody felt like arguing about points anymore.

"That was wild," Rolf said, grabbing the kickball to take it inside. "The Voice from the Spit Pit! Sounds like a ghost story."

"Yeah," I told him, "and my best kick of the year shoots back to haunt me. There ought to be a rule."

"Right," Rolf said. "Any pit ball returned by shovel counts triple."

"Hey, Rolf," Nick called, catching up with us. "I looked it up last night."

We both stared at him.

"The goldfish. I looked it up in the *Guinness Book of World Records*. And you were right. It was in there." Rolf shrugged and started to hurry on ahead like he didn't want to hear.

"No kidding," Nick went on, walking faster and catching Rolf by the elbow. "This is interesting. It says the book won't list records for 'potentially dangerous categories,' and that those are swallowing chewing gum, live ants, raw eggs in the shell, marshmallows—and goldfish."

"Marshmallows?" I asked. "What's potentially dangerous about marshmallows?"

"What's 'potentially dangerous'?" Rolf asked, his voice shaking a little.

"I think," Nick said, as we climbed the steps back to our room on the second floor, "I think that means it *could* kill you, but not for sure."

"Marshmallows?" I asked again.

"What if it doesn't stay swallowed long?" Rolf wanted to know.

"Oh, then it's perfectly safe," Nick told him, making it up for sure.

"Except for the goldfish," I said. "It couldn't have been very safe for the goldfish."

"Speaking of meals that won't stay down," Rolf interrupted, "when you gonna eat with Fearless Leader?"

"She says the day after Outdoor Ed because that's when her calendar has an empty space, but I'm gonna get out of it," I told him.

"Sounds potentially dangerous," he giggled.

31

"If we're late he'll *kill* us," Michelle was saying as she and Molly ran up the stairs behind us.

"No, he won't. He outlawed capital punishment," Molly told her, passing the three of us at a trot.

Actually, the city charter rules fined you a hundred dollars a minute for tardiness. We all made it to the room about fifty dollars after the bell. But Mr. Star didn't notice. He was standing at the front of the room talking to a pretty lady with thick black hair. We knew her. Her name is Svetlana Ivanovitch. And she is this wild sub who taught us two days in February while Mr. Star was out with the flu. She threw a wicked snowball, square danced like an Early American, and wasn't afraid to get her feet wet. Mr. Star had to talk down to her because he is over six feet tall and she is barely five. They were smiling and laughing, though, and couldn't have been thinking about us, late or not.

Miss Ivanovitch was wearing the same bell earrings she'd worn that day in February when we'd bet we could make her cry just by being awful. The earrings were jingling like crazy as she laughed at something Mr. Star told her.

"Jack," she asked, raising her dark eyebrows, "will we meet before then?"

Mr. Star nodded and handed her a big manila envelope.

"Jack?" Molly whispered to me, as we sank

32

back in our desks. *"Jack!* She called Mr. Star 'Jack'!"

"That's because Jack is his name," I explained.

"I *know* Jack is his name, but how does *she* know it?" She shifted nervously in her seat. "I don't like this one bit. They're *friends!"*

"They're so *cueshee* together," I heard Tracey tell Jenny. The girls make up these dumb words and then use them all the time. Cueshee means "cute."

"I love her green velvet skirt, don't you?"

"Yeah, and he's got that, like, darling dimple, and she's so—"

"Short," Molly said to them, leaning over the front of my desk. "She's much too short for him."

"She's taller than you are," Jenny said.

"Yes, but I'm going to grow and she's not. She's as high as she's ever going to get. And she's just all wrong for him. When I grow up—"

"He'll be married and have two kids," Eugene told her. "He must be at least twenty-five years old."

Molly turned her head away, flipping her hair especially far to show how much she thought of *that* idea. She raised her hand and, when Mr. Star didn't notice, started flapping it around. The drone in the class got louder.

"Mr. Star," Molly finally demanded, "what are we supposed to be doing?"

Mr. Star stopped talking to the sub. "My friends, you are supposed to be silent while I talk with our guest, Miss Ivanovitch, whom I think you all know."

She bobbed her head at us, her earrings pinging, to let us know *she* remembered.

Miss Ivanovitch hugged the big envelope Mr. Star had given her and said to us, "I *am* sorry to interrupt your lessons, but Mr. Star and I . . ." She looked up at him as though she'd just thought of something. "Mr. Star had some important papers for me. Perhaps I could tell you . . ." And she glanced up to Mr. Star to see if telling us was OK. When he nodded, she went on, "We're going to—"

"To get married," Molly gasped, turning to look at me in horror. As she turned, she knocked the gavel off her desk, and it clattered to the floor.

Miss Ivanovitch, startled, reached over to pick the gavel up, stepping, as she did, inside the taped-off section of Molly's property. According to class rules, that was trespassing unless you asked permission, or were invited, or like that.

"Miss Ivan-low-witch," Molly said sweetly, "you probably don't know it, but you're on private property."

Miss Ivanovitch, totally puzzled, pushed the hair out of her eyes with the handle of the gavel and looked to Mr. Star for an explanation.

"Molly," he said impatiently, "it should be

perfectly clear that Miss Ivanovitch is a visitor and—"

"I know," Molly told him with a little laugh. "I *do* apologize. It was just an automatic thing. Miss Ivan-slow-itch is an outsider. I'm sorry."

A lot of Miss Ivanovitch's bounce had disappeared, and she looked as though she wasn't sure she wanted to go on. But she took a deep breath and did.

"We are going to go on a trip together," she continued, skipping over Molly and smiling out at the rest of the class. She spread both her arms wide. Molly groaned. "All of us. Mr. Star and Miss Hutter have asked me to go with you to Wisconsin to learn about nature." She glanced back at Molly and smiled. "Isn't that wonderful!"

"Wonderful," Molly muttered, and, leaning back in her chair, she narrowed her eyes and folded her arms tight. "Just wonderful."

If One of Those Bottles Should Happen to Fall

SOMETIMES three weeks seems like forever, but those three whipped past so fast I didn't have time to catch a cold or sprain a toe. On the morning we were supposed to leave for camp I still hadn't made up a really good reason to stay home. Mom refused to buy my fever and sore throat. She took my temperature and made me say *Ah-ah-h-h-h*. My father growled from the bedroom that he had a bellyache, and when I said I did too, she opened the front door and waved me out. "Hobie Hanson, it's going to be a terrific trip," she said. I walked halfway down the steps and looked back at her without smiling.

That's when I saw the cat streak out between

her legs. Fido's an indoor cat, so I rushed over to trap him under the bushes.

"Leave him to me," she said. "The Rossis are ready to leave." So, even though my throat felt like it really might start to hurt at any minute, I climbed into the Rossis' car with my suitcase.

That's how I ended up at school marching to the camp bus at nine-fifteen, *laughing,* wondering if anybody else was dying to stay home.

Mrs. Rossi and the other mothers waved as we filed past. Two or three had babies strapped to their chests in kangaroo pouches. Toby was there, too.

"I want to go," he wailed. "I want to put a shark in Miss Hutter's sleeping bag." He yanked his mother forward by the knee of her jeans. "That was *last* year," Mrs. Rossi explained calmly. Then she reached over and stretched a wool cap over my head. "Your mother said to give this to you at the last minute so you wouldn't leave it behind," she told me. "And you're to wear it so you're sure to be well for your lunch with Miss Hutter on Thursday."

Toby howled. "This year," she explained to him, "they're going to be *good* at camp. You'll be happier at home."

It took two school buses to hold fifty-one kids with their duffles and suitcases. We had so many bags it looked like we were off for a year in Australia. Three kids stayed home sick. Nick said they were just scared to leave their teddy bears. I laughed and laughed, and my woollyworms started doing gymnastics in my stomach.

"Marshall, hold still!" Marshall stopped, embarrassed, and faced his mother's camera. Then he grabbed the guys around him and made us stay too. "OK, all four of you, smile!" she said.

Nick held two fingers up behind Marshall's head like they were horns. I stood totally in back of Nick except for one leg and one arm, which I stuck out so it looked like Nick had three of each. R.X. shoved one side of his face up and pulled the other down like it was made of Silly Putty.

Mrs. Ezry laughed and clicked the shutter. "Well, there's the Before picture. When you get back I'll take an After. Be good, now," she called as we climbed up the steps.

Nick and I sat in the second row of the front bus. The back bus had Ms. O'Malley in it with her 4A's and Mr. Plate, their student teacher from National College of Education. Miss Hutter and Mrs. Bosco were driving all the way to Camp Trotter so there'd be a car in case of emergency, and, I think, so they wouldn't have to ride with us.

Everyone was on our bus but Miss Ivanovitch, who stood searching up and down the sidewalk both ways like she was about to cross the street in heavy traffic, only there weren't any cars coming. She wore a purple check shirt, jeans that had a few miles on them, and hiking boots with major scars.

Mr. Star opened the window by his seat in the middle of the bus. "Come aboard," he called to her. "We're ready to roll."

She took a step back and checked behind both buses, then shifted her feet like she wasn't sure she wanted to leave.

Mr. Star called again. "We're all here," he said, "and accounted for."

Molly, who was sitting one row ahead and across the aisle from him, poked Lisa, who was next to her. "They're going to fight," she giggled.

"Maybe she's going to chicken out," Nick said, turning around in his seat and laughing with her. "She knows us." I laughed too. It felt pretty good to be laughing at someone.

So when Miss Ivanovitch finally climbed on the bus and the driver swooshed the doors closed, we were all breaking up over funny, purple, late Miss Ivanovitch.

She sat next to Mr. Star, stuffing her fancy embroidered purse under the seat, but he didn't bark at her for being late. He smiled.

As we pulled away, mothers called goodbye and Toby stood on his tiptoes, waving like crazy. Mrs. Ezry took a picture of the bus.

"Let's sing," Jenny yelled from the back.

"Let's not," Rolf called from the front.

Mr. Star and Miss Ivanovitch started talking. Jack and Svetlana. "Molly's jealous," Aretha said from the seat across from us.

"I am not," Molly leaned forward, whispering.

39

"I just happen to think she is totally wrong for him. They'd never ever be happy."

Miss I. and Mr. S. broke into this huge hysterical guffaw like one of them had told the all-time funny joke. Then Miss I. opened her flowery purse and offered him a mint, and he took it.

Molly sank down in her seat. Nick and I laughed out loud.

"You're absolutely right, Molly," Lisa said, looking straight over at me. "They'd probably

fight and end up getting divorced. It happens all the time. Michelle's parents are divorced. So are Rolf's. Mine are even thinking about it. It happens *all* the time." And it seemed like she was talking to me. I wondered what she knew.

The bus was rolling past my house. Was she talking about my folks? I stood up and wondered what I could do so they'd let me off.

"Down in front," Michelle said, and I sat.

It could be that those ladies at the fair knew something I didn't. They smiled like they felt really sorry for me. I felt sorry for me too.

In the back of the bus they were singing,

There was an old man named Michael
    Finnegan.
He had whiskers on his chinnegan.
Along came the wind and blew them in
    again.
Poor old Michael Finnegan. Begin again.

And they began again. And again.

I began to wonder if I'd left my bike outside. I
might have. If I did and my folks were getting a
divorce, they wouldn't see it out there turning
to rust. There were clouds and it looked like
rain.

I was half listening as Nick and R.X. and
Marshall started to sing,

Ninety-nine bottles of beer on the wall,
Ninety-nine bottles of beer—

Miss Ivanovitch jumped up and rushed over.
"Oh, my dears, don't," she said. "I can't travel
all the way to Wisconsin in a busful of broken
beer bottles. How about ninety-nine cans of
pop?"

"It won't sell," R.X. said. "Bottles of gin?"

She rolled her eyes. "Cartons of milk,
maybe?"

"Pitchers of spit?" Nick suggested.

"Oh, good grief," she laughed, turning back to
Mr. Star. "I give up."

If one of those pitchers should happen to
   fall
Ninety-five pitchers . . .

When I sang with them my flip-flopping woolly-worms dozed, and I decided this was going to be fun after all.

Rolf read signs out loud: " 'WOW Exotic Dancers,' 'FM 100, a Beautiful Place To Be,' 'Great America Theme Park, Second Right,' 'Filling Station Restaurant, Fabulous Food,' 'You are leaving Illinois, Land of Lincoln.' "

But we were still less than an hour away from school when Eugene hurried up from the back of the bus, tugged on Miss Ivanovitch's shirt, and said, "When are we going to be there?"

"Oh, ages," she told him. "We're not even halfway. We'll be there in about ninety minutes."

"I don't feel so good," he whispered, and she got up and followed him to the back of the bus.

As soon as she left, Molly moved over to Miss Ivanovitch's seat.

"How about a page or two of Mad Libs, Mr. Star?" she asked.

"I'm game," he told her. "Shoot."

Molly smiled over at us. "Adjective?"

"Peaceful," he said with a sigh.

After we'd stopped at the side of the road for Eugene to get sick in the bushes, we started passing more plain hills than billboard ones.

43

There was a huge blackbird sitting in the top of a tree with no leaves, a pick-your-own-strawberries farm that was closed because it wasn't strawberry season yet, great green lakes around almost every curve, and lots of black-and-white cows that Michelle said were cueshee and Aretha said were Holsteins.

"What are we going to do up there?" Marshall came over and asked Nick. "I mean *do*. Last year's fourth grade got famous for Outdoor Ed. You want to plan ahead or shall we just make it up as we go along?"

Nick reached into the small paper bag he'd brought on the bus and opened it up a crack so Marshall and I could look inside. A hairy, warty, gangrene-gray rubber hand lay limp in the bottom of the sack, ready to pick up and wave at night through somebody's open window. I felt like it was already dark, and I wished I was home with my blue striped sheets pulled over my head. And my mom and dad listening to the *Late Evening News*. And then I remembered that my dad hadn't said goodbye and that the cat was lost and my bike dead or stolen. My hands began to sweat.

Beep-beep-beep-beep-beep—beep-beep! The bus driver honked to announce we had arrived at Camp Trotter. The sun was shining now, and the cap I'd forgotten I was wearing was much too hot.

"I'm starving," R.X. called as the bus ground

44

to a stop. "It's eleven thirty-seven—when do they feed us?"

We climbed out and gathered around while the driver opened the back door of the bus and handed out bags. Tracey, the littlest kid in our class, had a suitcase with wheels on it. She tried to pull it along the gravel by its strap, but it fell over on its side like a stubborn dog. My things were in a little red suitcase of my mother's. You could tell those kids who'd been to camp before. They had scruffy duffles that looked like they'd been stored in caves.

I followed Mr. Star up the steps to the long stone building we'd be staying in. He was carrying two suitcases—his and *hers*. At the landing he picked some guy's underwear off the tip of the Camp Trotter sign, dropped it in the trash barrel, and barked, straight at me, "Don't get any ideas, my friend."

"Where are we going now?" Eugene asked, looking pale still.

"I don't know," Marshall said, resting his long khaki duffle on the lodge's porch railing. "But I gotta get there fast. It feels like I've got two dogs and a cat in here."

Even though they'd shown us a map and told us ahead of time who we were rooming with and where, it was a madhouse inside. Miss Ivanovitch had rushed ahead of the mob and was stationed in the front hall, handing everybody who came in two white sheets, a pillowcase, and a towel. "I want to see snappy hospital corners on your beds," she told us all. Mr. Plate, next to her, shouted out room numbers to people who'd forgotten. I went searching for room nine.

"Hey, you guys," Rolf yelled, tromping down the steps. "Room nine is next to the girls' shower. A room with a view. Can you believe it?"

"Don't believe it," Miss Ivanovitch called. "Upstairs is the girls' floor. Boys are downstairs."

As we headed into the real room nine, Rolf and I bumped into Nick rushing out. "I'm not going to sleep in that smelly place," he said, brushing past us. "I'm going to complain." When we walked in and looked around, I thought it smelled good, damp and musty, like our basement after a good rain.

The room was small, with two dressers and two double-decker beds, a blanket folded on each. Nick's stuff was piled on one of the top bunks. I threw my red bag on the top of the other. Rolf sat down on the bed under Nick's and sank about eight inches.

"What's a hospital corner?" he asked.

I climbed on my top bunk and tried to fold the neat, sharp corners like my dad had made in the Army and taught me how. Except I wonder how people make top bunks. With my suitcase and my feet at one end, I spread out the sheet and tucked in the corners, crawled to the other end, pushed

46

the suitcase behind me and tried to pull the sheet straight. But I was on top of it and it wouldn't pull. When I tried jumping in the air and yanking at the same time, all I did was bang my head on the ceiling. My bed looked like a plate of spaghetti.

"Doesn't look so great from underneath," Rolf said. "Look, don't tell anybody, but I never made a bed before."

"Well, then, don't worry about hospital corners." I hopped down and tried to stuff the sheets in any old way. "It's no big deal."

"Room check in ten minutes," Mr. Star shouted as he walked down the hall. "I want those beds so I can bounce a quarter on them."

"Why would he want to bounce a quarter on a bed?"

"To show it's tight like a trampoline. That's supposed to be good. My dad says—" I told him, and suddenly remembered that my dad had hardly eaten anything or said anything at supper the night before, and he's a big eater and a big talker. I didn't know why I hadn't figured it out before. Lisa said her folks were talking about a divorce. I never knew *that* before, either. Probably, I decided, there were a lot of things I didn't know.

"I've got to call home," I said. "I forgot something."

"That's against the rules," Rolf told me. "What'd you forget?"

It was twelve fifteen and nobody would be home anyway except the cat, and he was probably somewhere in Ohio crying in the top of a tree. I shrugged. "I guess it's no big deal."

"They *all* smell like this," Nick said, rushing in and vaulting onto his bed. "We'll just have to open the windows."

Eugene dragged his suitcase in, plunked his things on the bed under mine, and went silently to work while Rolf watched him spread, tuck, and fold.

"I never made a bed before," Rolf explained to Eugene and Nick. "Don't tell anybody." I think he wanted us to feel sorry for him and make it ourselves.

"Well, you better do it now or Mr. Star will send you home," Nick told him.

"Really?" Eugene asked brightly, dumping his pillow back out of its case.

"No, not really, but we can't eat till they're made, and I'm starved." I watched him stuff the hairy hand and a flashlight under his pillow.

Rolf spread his sheets and blanket kitty-corner on his bed, tucked some in, and then pulled a bag of stuff out of his suitcase and set it on the crumpled blanket.

"You want to see clever?" Rolf asked us. "I decided to beat last year's guys and their fat-fish-in-the-bed trick. You know that list they gave us, 'Articles To Bring' and 'Articles To Be Left at

48

Home'?" He whipped it out and said proudly, "I brought *all* the Articles To Be Left at Home."

He waved a cellophane-wrapped package of peanut butter and crackers at us. "Number one. Food." Then he opened up a small sack and poured out a heap of Hubba Bubba. "Number two. Gum." He flopped out an *Archie*. "Number three. Comic books." An *Archie!* "Number four. Radios." He turned a switch on something that looked exactly like a Pepsi can, only it crackled with static and a faint echo of music. "Five. Money." He flipped two quarters onto the bed. They didn't bounce. "And I'm counting the plastic spreader in the peanut butter and crackers as number six, knives. The only thing I didn't bring was number seven, a tape recorder, because I don't actually have one. Good stuff, huh?"

We were still deciding how to answer that when Mr. Star blasted through the door. "What ho!" he said. "This may well be the messiest room on my beat. And what's more, I believe I see an entire stack of contraband. I shall confiscate it and return it to its rightful owner when we arrive home." He scooped it up and dumped it all into its original sack. "Yours, I presume, Rolf?"

"Mine, Mr. Star," he sighed.

An enormous cackley laugh rang out as a bell from the mess hall down the hill called us to lunch. It was Mrs. Bosco's laugh. And it was close by.

49

"Oh, I'll keep an eye on them. Don't you worry," she was saying. "They won't put anything, *anything* over on me." And she cackled again. Mrs. Bosco was in the room next to ours, no doubt about it. On the boys' floor. Mrs. Bosco was keeping her eye on *us*.

4

Rip

"Yuck, this stuff looks like imitation Central School food," Tracey groaned as she plopped the bowl of macaroni casserole on our table. She wore a white chef's cap, which meant she was our table's "hopper," the one who goes to the kitchen for food.

"It looks like a lovely dish," Miss Hutter said when it was passed to her, still untouched. She lifted a heaping spoonful onto her plate. There was probably tuna in it. For sure there was celery.

"That's what I meant," Tracey said. "Lovely."

Dishes of chocolate pudding and a plate of carrot sticks were already on the table when we sat down, so most people ate pudding first, even

51

though Miss Hutter pointed out that it wasn't a good appetizer.

"Pass the peanut butter, jelly, and bread," R.X. called when Tracey arrived with them. She had to go back for thirds for the p.b. and j., and R.X. must have eaten a whole loaf of bread. But the casserole just sat there with one cave in it. Even Miss Hutter didn't take seconds. I couldn't swallow anything. The fuzzy creatures in my stomach had taken up tap dancing.

"Hey, Hobie," Rolf whispered from the next table, "you practicing up for your fancy schmancy lunch Thursday?" He pointed at Miss Hutter and laughed behind his hand. Big deal.

Out the mess hall windows we could see across Lake Lindaloma and the rows of big old houses on the other side. Two orange pontoon boats bobbed in the waves at the dock. I guess it was too early for water skiers.

Soon Mr. Star stood up, raised his hand, and shouted, "OK, friends. I can't talk unless everybody is listening. So let's cease conversation."

At the next table Molly stopped nibbling carrot sticks long enough to lean over and ask Miss Ivanovitch, "Have you ever noticed how mean Mr. Star can be? It's something you realize the longer you know him. He's basically a very mean person."

"OK, friends," Mr. Star went on, "when you finish, pass your plates to the hopper, who'll clean the table." Groans from the hoppers. Laughs from everyone else. "Those of you who are laughing will get your chance. And when you get back to your room make sure your bed is well made, because you'll want to collapse on it when we come back from the cemetery. It's a long way."

"Cemetery? Is he kidding?" a kid from 4A asked me. Miss Hutter stared him down. Mr. S. had warned us about the walk to the cemetery.

"And make sure you go to the bathroom. There aren't any toilets along the way to the graveyard."

Nick and I were the first ones out. We ran from the mess hall by the lake back to the lodge and swept through the girls' rooms upstairs, where we saw pink rabbits, Paddington bears, little heart pillows, one large stuffed donkey, a gray cat with a red ribbon, and a nightgown printed with "Numero Uno."

Rushing down the steps before the teachers or Mrs. Bosco came, we climbed fast into our top bunks so if they said, Was it you on the girls' floor, we'd say, No, I'm asleep. Nobody asked, so we played catch with the hairy rubber hand until it was time to leave.

Mrs. Bosco and Miss Hutter didn't go with us to the cemetery. As we left, I heard Mrs. Bosco shout to Miss Hutter, "I'm glad I'm not going with them right after lunch. When they eat, all the juices go straight to their little stomachs, you know, leaving their brains completely empty. Completely empty. It's a scientific fact.''

The cemetery was almost a mile away, and we set off down the side of the road single file, in four big groups, each group with a teacher-type leader. Mine got Miss Ivanovitch. Or she got us, I'm not sure which. She called our group the Scotch Tape because, she said, she wanted us to stick together. That's better than being called the Lindalomas, which is what Ms. O'Malley's was. Mr. Star's kids named themselves the CIA, for Central's Intelligence Agency, and Mr. Plate's group was the Bowls. Seven of the Scotch Tape were from Mr. Star's class: Nick, Marshall, Eugene, Molly, Lisa, Aretha, and me. The others were 4A: Lynda, Elizabeth, Cindy, Stewart, Vince, and Glen.

About seven hundred fifty years later we got there. Two dogs had snarled at us, and a black-and-white cat followed us when we said, ''Here, kitty, kitty.'' I wondered who Fido had followed. Ms. O'Malley passed word back that if we touched the flags on the outdoor mailboxes we would be committing a federal offense and probably spend six to eight months in the penitentiary. And Lisa's new shoes had rubbed blisters on her heels, so the Scotch Tape had to walk slow to keep back with her.

Miss Ivanovitch kept jogging ahead and waiting. "Come on, Tape," she called from the cemetery gate. "These folks can't hurt you. . . ."

Eugene sat down inside the entrance and refused to budge.

It was spooky. Dark clouds were rolling over, and so was a thin layer of fog. We crept slowly around, trying to fill in all the blanks on the mimeographed sheets they'd given us asking who was buried in the oldest grave and which stones were made of granite, which of sandstone, and whether there were families that died all at once. (There was one—the Needlings whose last dates were all June 14, 1879, only it didn't say why.) Stars stood for people who were killed in wars.

And there was a baby angel on a gravestone, a cherub Miss Ivanovitch liked. The stone read "Luella Winston, Died April 4, 1858, 3 weeks, 4 days old." Miss Ivanovitch sank to her knees in front of it and called, "Jack, this is the one I want to do a rubbing of. This one will be perfect for our new hall."

"Aha," Nick said. "Our new hall."

Mr. Star gathered all four groups around and handed out big sheets of white paper and black crayons. Ms. O'Malley explained how to rub the crayon flat on the paper to get the gravestone's picture to appear. I'd done it before lots of times, rubbing a pencil over a paper-covered penny, so I knew what she was talking about.

Miss Ivanovitch told us not to get crayon on

the gravestones and set to work on her cherub. When Nick and I said we didn't know what to rub, she told us to find letters from different tombstones and spell out our own names. But that got to be pretty eerie when we thought about it.

We had sat down on two humps that were dead people when Nick spotted Molly and Lisa heading our way. We hid behind big stones marked Beucher, making ourselves as small as possible and quiet as corpses. Balancing on our toes, we waited, ready to leap out and grab them by the ankles as they passed.

But just at the instant we were going to pounce, we got grabbed ourselves—by the ribs. Michelle and Jenny had seen us hide and crept up as silent as Indians. We weren't afraid, of course, it's just that when you get grabbed by the ribs, you naturally yell.

But they wouldn't let it go. "Scaredy cat, dirty rat, don't know what you're looking at!" They danced like spirits in the night, waving their rubbings and howling like werewolves. And just then the wind whipped up the rain in little misty drops. We could hear it on the leaves before we felt it. I zipped my jacket up and half wished I hadn't left my cap in the room.

"Look at this," Miss Ivanovitch said proudly, her hair blowing like a big black bush around her head. She held up her rubbing of the angel, and it was good. She hadn't moved the paper as she rubbed like we did, so nothing was smudged. You could see the baby's smile, and all the letters were clear. "Hold this for me while I get organized, will you?" she asked, handing up the rubbing and scrambling to her feet.

I grabbed and Nick grabbed and we both got it. I got one half and he got the other. The damp paper split right down the middle.

Miss Ivanovitch's face lost all its joy, and we knew that our "I'm sorry's" weren't going to help.

"*Why* did you have to do that!" she said, tilting her head both ways to look at the damage. "I *really* wanted it and I was pleased with the funny grin the angel had and . . ." She tried to pull her hair back from the wind. Nick gave her his half of the rubbing. She shrugged, rolled it up, and stuffed it into her raincoat pocket.

I was going to hand her my half too, but a blast of wind lifted the paper away, flipped it past an evergreen, and plastered it flat against Albert, son of M. and S. Matfield, died April 5, 1849.

"Oh, just toss it in the trash," she said, and ran to join the other teachers. I felt awful. She was really mad. When Miss I. showed them the torn paper, Mr. Star put his hand on her shoulder and looked really pained. He didn't turn to chew us out, though, so she must not have told him how it happened.

The girls went crazy when he touched her.

Miss I. and Mr. S. walked together on the way

Luella Winston
Died April 3, 185?
4 days old

back, a row of girls lined up to trail behind them. Nobody cared about groups anymore.

Aretha stopped, picked up a long stick from the side of the road, and wrote in the damp dirt, "J.S. + S.I." Jenny, who was walking with her, drew a heart around it.

"He's tall and she's short," Molly announced. "He's blond and she's got black curly hair. He's nice and she's dwerpy. Their children would be freaks."

"My father's blond and *my* mother's brunette," Jenny said.

"That's what I meant," Molly answered, shuffling through the heart like she was doing a war dance.

I rolled the torn angel up with the rubbing I'd made of my name. "Think we could stick it together with tape?" I asked Nick.

"You got any?"

I shrugged. "She said she wanted it for her new hall, too."

"Our new hall, that's what it was. And who do you think 'our' is?" he asked with a grin like he knew who.

"You mean you think she *is* going to marry Mr. Star?"

"Looks like it. He carried her suitcase."

"That's because she had to run ahead to hand out sheets and towels."

"Maybe," he said, shrugging his shoulders. "You know what I think we ought to do?" he

59

asked. "I think we ought to make another rubbing for her—for them." One of the dogs who'd growled at us on the way ran up to sniff our feet. "Would they let us go back to the cemetery now?"

"No, it's going to rain too hard." The sky rumbled as if to say, That's right, fella.

"Tomorrow?"

"They've got stuff for us to do all day."

"Tomorrow night?"

"In the dark?"

"It gets dark at night."

"We could take turns rubbing. And give it to them as a wedding present."

"We'd better take a good look around at how to get there if we're going to go back at night." It was one straight road. No way to get lost.

We were the last of the line. Even Lisa and her blisters had moved on ahead because she was carrying her shoes.

The black-and-white cat padded up behind us, going, "Me-*owl*. Me-*owl*."

Nick kneeled down to it and said, "No, dummy, you no *owl*. Owls go hoot in the night. You *cat*."

"Me-*owl*," it said again, not believing Nick for a minute.

I scratched the owl cat's neck the way Fido liked me to do, then picked it up and carried it back to the lodge under my jacket. It was warm and had a purr so loud I sounded like I ran on batteries.

As we got to the porch the sky filled with a white-blue flash, and the thunder began to rumble through our bones. Mr. Plate, who was in charge of a crate of apples in the big front hall, handed us each one. In their rooms kids were talking and laughing.

We bit into our apples and listened for a minute at the bottom of the girls' steps. If we'd really wanted to, we could have dashed to the top like we had after lunch. Mr. Plate was leaning out the front door, taking deep breaths of the electric air and watching the storm move in. We could have. But we didn't. Instead, I opened my jacket and let loose on the girls one black-and-white cat who thought he was an owl.

Zap

THE rain held off, with the clouds growling a lot but not biting, so they marched us back outside to play matching games with a batch of rocks that all looked the same to me. Molly matched her granite with my granite, which I thought for sure was quartz. And then we played kickball two games at a time on a wide, wide, open field with no fences. The ball kept lifting off and drifting away with the wind, no matter how is was thrown or kicked, and Miss Ivanovitch made two freaky home runs. Back at our playground a ball couldn't go spinning off like that into the middle distance. But then, at school teachers didn't play kickball, either.

If we'd been at school, really, it would have

been out and I would have been at home watching TV before supper. Camp Trotter didn't have a TV. For sure I wouldn't have been matching rocks with Molly Bosco or listening to Lisa Soloman talk about how this darling lost cat took a flying leap into her upper bunk.

The later it got, the more like home it wasn't.

"Icky chicken," Tracey said when R.X., who was supper hopper, brought a bowl of it to our table. Tracey said she never ate green beans because they gave her a rash, and she took only a mound of mashed potatoes, which she raked with her fork. Some kids who had treated lunch like an art project wolfed down supper. Graveyards and groundballs make you hungry. I even ate some, trying not to think about the night ahead. R.X., though, was gross. He stuffed whole pieces of bread into his mouth and chewed puff-cheeked, yawning now and then to make the kids across from him sick. When Miss Hutter looked, he always tried to have his mouth shut and his eyes staring up at the ceiling, innocent.

"R.X., I can't believe you eat this way at home," Miss Hutter told him. He smiled, his lips sealed.

After supper some of us walked down to the lake and tried skipping a few stones—granite, marble, rubies, whatever. The waves, pushed high by the wind, ate all the stones before the third skip, even Marshall's, and he threw like a pro.

63

On the way back to the lodge the rain began to fall—sideways, because the gusts were so strong. We ran, crunching pebbles under our feet.

When the hoppers were all back from cleaning and scrubbing the tables, we gathered in the big recreation room upstairs on the girls' floor. One wall was windows looking out over the lake. Another was stone—wall-stone probably—with a fireplace in it filled with logs that weren't burning.

Ms. O'Malley was showing off a batch of the day's rubbings. But a lot of kids were rolling around on the floor, shrieking, so she and Mr. Star tried to organize us into our groups again. They made us sit with no talking at all for one whole minute by the clock on the wall. Mr. Plate grinned like it was really funny, but a minute is a long time. The clock said seven-seventeen when we shut our mouths and seven-eighteen when we could open them again. In the first fifteen seconds I thought about how my bike was out in the back of my house, rusting away to crust. In the second fifteen seconds I could see Fido soaked to the skin, crying for me. By thirty seconds I was watching my mother wave goodbye forever to my father, an umbrella keeping the lightning away. The mashed potatoes in my stomach had turned to plaster.

It was getting dark.

Miss Ivanovitch, Miss Hutter, and Mrs. Bosco hurried into the room together. Miss Ivanovitch and Miss Hutter could tell what was going on. Mrs. Bosco couldn't hear the silence.

"Well, Svetlana," she bellowed, "I'm *so* happy for you. We're *all* so very happy for you."

Miss Ivanovitch turned red and sank to the floor with the Scotch Tape. Mrs. Bosco had changed into new very blue jeans and a sweatshirt that said Iowa State. She settled herself on the flowered sofa against the wall across from the fireplace. Miss Hutter, still in her red suit with the little striped bow at the neck, sat with her.

"Why do you suppose we're all supposed to be so happy for Miss Ivanovitch?" Nick asked with a grin.

"Because she had no cavities at her last checkup," I told him.

Other people were whispering the same question, but nobody asked Miss Ivanovitch. Instead, the girls, except for Molly and Lisa, all rearranged themselves on the floor until they got Miss Ivanovitch next to Mr. Star. It wasn't all that easy to do, either, because a nature person from Camp Trotter was trying to wade through us holding a projector over his head like we were water that would ruin it. He was going to be our evening class.

"OK, you guys. Coming through. Coming through," he growled. "Let's see a little consideration here. Can't you keep these kids quiet?" he called to Mr. Star, even though we weren't making all that much noise. Mostly it was whispering. Mr. Star looked like he'd half a mind to send the guy to the principal for a good chewing out. But he stopped fuming and grinned when Miss Ivanovitch whispered something in his ear. Molly moved in closer.

We waited on the floor in the half dark while the guy with the slides got plugged in. The exit signs glowed red in front of us. Before long the nature person was telling us what the Old Greeks thought about the sky and about constellations, but out the window behind him all we could see was thick black stripes across murky gray. There were no stars.

When the slide show started, Rolf stuck his hands up to make a rabbit on the screen. Mr. Star sent him to sit on the sofa, sandwiched between Mrs. Bosco and Miss Hutter. Everybody laughed but Rolf.

The guy finished his first round of slides with a picture of an astronaut's footsteps on the moon. He was putting another set in the projector when a blast of lightning exploded like somebody taking our picture with a giant flash cube. The thunder cracked so fast that the bolt must have grazed the window. The air smelled funny.

A lot of people yelled. Eugene, who was sitting in front of Miss Hutter's knees, started to cry. She leaned over and talked close to his ear.

Mr. Star got up, stepped over the kids around him, and flicked on the lights. "Intermission," he said, easy, as though nothing had happened. "Everybody stretch."

"Now, don't you worry, children," Mrs. Bosco shouted as she rose from the sofa. "It never strikes twice in the same place. Never. And that's a scientific fact."

The lightning blinded us again.

Its blast followed before I could count one.

"Did you know there's a restaurant on the moon?" Miss Ivanovitch asked as we were all sitting down again. I glanced at the guy with the slides, who looked annoyed.

"Why, no, Miss Ivanovitch," Nick answered. "Tell us about the restaurant on the moon."

"Well," she said, waiting till everything but the night was quiet, "it has great food, but absolutely no atmosphere." Some kids laughed, some groaned, some asked other kids next to them what it meant, but the awful, scary feeling was gone.

And that's when the lights went out. Even the red exit lights.

Everybody screamed. The room sounded like a roller coaster halfway down its first fall.

"OK, pull it back together," Mr. Star shouted.

Miss Ivanovitch stood up. And when the howls hit bottom, she asked, "Do you all have flashlights in your rooms?" Most of us did. They were on the Articles To Bring list.

So when the projector guy headed out to fix the plug, or whatever, Miss Hutter and Mr. Plate stuck around to shush us, and the rest of the adult types went out flashlight hunting.

They weren't gone long. Each one had two for good measure.

"I expect this is really all we'll need," Miss Ivanovitch was saying as they came in. "After all, we're not having a supermarket grand opening."

We huddled together like it was cold, listening to the blasts outside. The sky had gone crazy.

"Actually," Mr. Star told us, raising his voice over the sound effects, "we were going to turn the lights out anyway."

I could hear Eugene breathing raspy in his throat. Rolf had slid off the sofa when Mrs. Bosco and Miss Hutter left. He moved in close to Nick and me.

"You know how we've been talking about animals of the woods in school? Well," Mr. Star said, "most mammals—about eighty-five percent of all mammals—are awake and roving at night."

"Geez," Rolf whispered. "What a bore. Do we have to learn *all* the time?"

"How do they find each other in the dark?" Mr. Star asked.

The night outside turned day again, but this lightning was farther away than the last.

"That's how," a kid yelled, and everybody laughed.

"Very bright," Mr. Star said. He stuck the

flashlight under his chin so it made shadows on his face like he was the Teacher Monster.

"Lightning bugs flicker," a girl said.

"And do it without thunder," the Teacher Monster nodded.

"Crickets make noises," another voice said.

"Very sound." He flashed his beam over the group, looking for more answers.

"Dogs *smell* stuff out," Michelle called.

Mr. Star aimed his light at her.

"So do sharks," Rolf yelled, and the flash landed on him. "They smell blood in the water."

"True," Mr. Star said. "Even in the dark." He snapped off his light.

The lightning had stopped, but it was still raining. There were probably no sharks in Lake Lindaloma. And the water hadn't gotten deep enough for them to snap at the windows anyway.

The other teachers and Mrs. Bosco turned off their flashlights, and we talked about how we would find each other blind.

"There are predators out there now, animals searching for food, for their prey. Each one must be careful not to be caught. We are going to play a game in the dark called Predator-Prey." I got goose bumps on my arms.

The adults, holding turned-on flashlights, moved through the kids, handing out stuff. Some kids got sandpaper blocks to scrape together like in rhythm bands. Some got penlights to flash.

Rolf had a Kleenex soaked in perfume that smelled like roses, and Miss Ivanovitch gave me a baby food jar with some stones in it.

"OK, you guys," Mr. Star explained, "there are four kinds of prey in this game: scrapers, lights, rattles, and roses."

"P.U.," a kid called.

"That's *my* perfume, sonny," Mrs. Bosco said from the sidelines.

"As soon as one rattler finds another rattler, one rose another rose, and so forth, both are safe," Mr. Star went on. "When you've found another creature like you, move close to a wall and sit down out of everybody's way. You are the prey." That was me—a rattler.

"OK, but four of you out there are wearing black T-shirts. You are the predators, out for your evening meal. One of you eats only the rose creatures, and so forth. When you predators meet one of your prey, tap him—or her—on the shoulder, say 'Zap!' in his ear—"

"Or hers," Molly said. "And you've made your kill."

"Exactly."

Next to me, Eugene was pulling a predator shirt on over his head.

In the total dark and almost total silence, we mixed ourselves up in the room, like shuffled cards. Some kids, you could tell, were holding onto each other, cheating.

"Do you think he'll kiss her?" I heard Jenny whisper to somebody as she passed. "It's romantic in the dark."

"It is *not* romantic," Molly answered. "Besides, he'd probably miss. She's such a Munchkin."

"Predators, I hope you're ready," Mr. Star announced from over near the door. "Your prey are about to start roaming through the night woods. I'm going to give you sixty seconds in the dark." He turned a penlight on his wristwatch. "Ready, set, *go!*"

We whirled around, sniffing, shaking, scraping, and blinking. I caught onto somebody who rattled at me. It was Marshall, and we collapsed near the fireplace, glad not to be eaten. When the sixty seconds was up, the teachers turned on all eight flashlights. And we saw that nine kids had been captured. Five of them were flashlights. Two were scrapers. Two were perfume. Not a single rattle had been caught. Eugene was the rattle predator. I guess they made him one to make him feel strong. But it didn't work.

"Hey, Eugene," Rolf yelled, "You're a real tiger."

We mixed up the jars and scratchers and stuff and played a few more times with different predators. "Zap!" you'd hear in the dark and "Zap!" again. Kids got smarter about not flashing lights too long and all, but anybody who'd ever had the perfumed Kleenex smelled like it the whole time.

As we dropped the stuff into cardboard boxes and sat down again, Miss Ivanovitch lit the logs in the fireplace. The twigs began to crackle. It was scary in the total dark, but lonelier when the fire was burning. I missed home again. And nobody else seemed to be jumpy but Eugene.

Mrs. Bosco stepped up next to the fireplace. Now she was wearing a huge gray sweater with big lumpy pockets over her Iowa State sweatshirt. She leaned toward us. "I am going to tell you a tale," she said, slow and mysterious. The fire was so bright you could see almost the whole room. It was reflected in the windows, so there were two fires and two Mrs. Boscos.

"Once," she began, "in the deep, dark past, there was a monkey's paw." And she told us this really bizarre story about a guy who got ground up in a machine at work because his parents wished for money with this magic monkey's paw. First they wished for two thousand dollars or something, and the insurance money for his getting ground up was two thousand dollars, so they got their money, only then they didn't want it. Anyway, they used the second wish from this monkey's paw to bring him back to life, only when he came back that night he was still all ground up, so they had to use up their third wish to get him dead again because how are you going

to sit down with your family for supper if you're all ground up? Actually, it was a gross and excellent story. And even though she is Molly's grandmother, she did a good job of telling it.

But when she announced that she was going to tell another, Miss Hutter said, "Oh, no, I think one ghost story is quite enough tonight." She probably thought it would keep us awake and scared, but that story was nothing to the stuff on TV. It didn't matter, anyway, because Mrs. Bosco didn't hear a word Miss Hutter said. And when everybody started to clap for her to tell the other one, she did.

The fire threw moving shadows across us and smelled of the woods. Mrs. Bosco hunched up her shoulders and began slowly in a deep, dark voice. "It was," she began quietly, "a deep, dark, stormy night . . . in a deep, dark, enchanted forest." She waited for the rumble of faraway thunder to stop. "And in that deep, dark, enchanted forest, there was a deep, dark, haunted graveyard. And in that deep, dark, and haunted graveyard, there was a deep, dark, yawning hole. And in that deep, dark, yawning hole . . ." Her voice got lower and quieter and quivered a little. ". . . there was a deep . . . dark . . . moldy . . . box." She stopped and said nothing for about fifteen seconds. "And in that deep . . . dark . . . moldy box . . ."

She reached into the pocket of her sweater.

". . . there was a *monkey's paw!*" She waved a furry clawlike thing at us, and everybody screamed.

When she rubbed Michelle's cheek with the paw, I saw what it was. It was Nick's hairy hand, shimmering like real in the flicker of the light.

Honk

Nick was mad.

"She *stole* it," he said, back in the room, cradling the creepy paw in his hands. "She stole it when she got my flashlight. And now I can't use it to scare anybody because everybody knows."

"It's an awful hand, even when you know," I said, watching him wobble it. "Maybe you could try making three wishes."

He tossed it to me. "You try," he said.

I wish I was home, I thought automatically, since that's what I'd been wishing ever since we'd left. The paw moved in my hand. I swear. "I take that back," I said out loud, and threw the paw to Eugene.

"I wish the lights would go on," he said.

Three flashlights, like torches, lit our room.

76

Rolf's batteries had burnt out, so his was back in the suitcase. Because we couldn't go running up to kids flapping the old hand at them, we threw pillows at each other instead and moved our beds closer together so we could lie across like bridges.

There was a pay phone in the front hall where Mr. Plate had stood to give us apples. I didn't have any money, but I remembered what my dad had told me once about calling collect if I was desperate.

I was desperate. I wasn't going to be able to sleep if I couldn't call home. So I headed, with my flashlight off, straight into the dark.

"Going to the john," I announced as I left.

Rolf said to wait up, but I moved as quickly as I could with one hand on the wall. I decided it was safer to travel with my flashlight off. If they couldn't find me, they couldn't stop me. I edged along toward where I thought the phone was, shuffling slowly, my bare feet cold on the boards. I ran flat into a wall where I didn't think there was one, so I flicked on my flash until I spotted the phone. Nobody arrested me.

Kids were still yelling in their rooms, and I could see beams of light dancing around the girls' stairs as they passed by at the top.

I stood quietly, listening for footsteps and watching for lights. I'd never made a call like this before, and for all I knew it couldn't really be done for free. So I picked up the receiver, turned my light on the dial, and pushed the O for Opera-tor. I told her what I wanted to do, but, since it was a long distance call, she gave me a lot of numbers and when I started to push them I couldn't remember the right order. I hung up. What if I called Moscow by mistake?

I punched O again. A man answered this time, and I tried harder to remember. Aiming my light on the numbers, I pushed 1-312-212-2786. Some-body, not my mother, answered, "May I help you?" I explained I wanted to call home and have my parents pay and she said, "Your name?" And I told her, Hobie Hanson, their son.

The phone at the other end rang and rang and rang and rang. Fifteen times I counted, but no-body answered. My parents were always tired after work. They never went places on Monday nights. It must have been time for the ten o'clock news. They were out looking for the cat. They were chasing the guy who stole my bike. No, they had both moved away forever.

I didn't hang up the phone. I just let the re-ceiver swing loose, ringing. My eyes were sting-ing. I felt like a baby.

Nick and Rolf are going to wonder if I've fallen in, I thought, and I started to feel my way back to the room, the phone buzzing behind me. As I slid my hand along the wall, I suddenly got this in-credibly eerie feeling all the way down to my toes. Someone else's hand was on top of mine, sliding. We both gasped.

"Who are you?" a voice whispered. And that's when Eugene's wish was granted. All of the lights, all over the place, went on. It was so bright it hurt your eyes like the sun.

Miss Ivanovitch looked at me like I'd just stepped off a UFO. "What are you doing here, Hobie?" She was wearing a bathrobe of the fuzzy brown stuff they make teddy bears out of.

I swallowed hard. "Taking a walk," I said. "How about you?"

"Me, too." She stared at me for a minute, frowned, and then reached out and wiped a tear off my cheek. I pushed her hand away, so she stuck both of them in her pockets. One of them came right back out with some coins in it.

"Actually, I'm going to use the telephone," she said. "It's not against the rules for adults."

The phone was still ringing, and we both could hear it.

"I tried my folks but nobody was there."

"Homesick?" she asked, gently.

"I forgot something." Trying to explain, I said, "The cat ran away. Also, I think my folks are getting a divorce." I shrugged. "Nobody answers. I guess they've both left." And no matter how hard I tried, I couldn't keep my eyes dry. "I want to go home," I told her.

She bit her lip and looked at me for a while. "Hobie, I wish I could just tell you everything's OK, but I don't know if it is," she said. "But, whatever, it'll wait until Wednesday. It's waited this long." She walked over to a grocery sack on the floor and brought out a big bag of marshmallows.

"We were going to roast these tonight in the fire," she said, "but we figured it wouldn't be safe with all those sticks in the pitch dark."

"Potentially dangerous," I said, with a little laugh, remembering the *Guinness Book of World Records*. I popped a marshmallow into my mouth and chewed. The sweet, soft goo of it was wonderful. She probably wouldn't understand if I pretended it was poisoning me.

"Why, Hobie, I had no idea you had such an impressive vocabulary. Your parents must be very proud of you."

"I do want to go home," I told her. "Please. Isn't there some way?"

"Not unless you could get Mrs. Bosco to drive you, and then you'd have to have a pretty good reason."

"I don't want to talk to Mrs. Bosco about it."

"Then you're going to have to hang in there."

On the floor near the phone the snack box had an apple left in it from the afternoon. I reached over, grabbed it, and fled back to the room.

All the kids who'd tried to go to bed earlier when the lights were out were up now, wandering the rooms like it was morning.

"What took you?" Rolf asked. "I had to borrow Nick's flashlight."

"I was starving, so I stole an apple," I told him, stuffing it in my mouth whole, like I was a roast pig.

Nick was pressing something against the ceiling light.

"It's a glow-in-the-dark Frisbee," he said. "My flashlight wouldn't charge it enough."

Eugene wasn't there.

"He went whimpering off to Mr. Star," Rolf said. "What a baby."

"Really?" I asked, wondering if my eyes looked all red and my cheeks striped.

Mr. Star, Mrs. Bosco, and Mr. Plate were all calling, "Lights out."

"Again?" I yelled. "We're just getting used to them."

Eugene hurried back in, staring at his feet, so I couldn't look for tear streaks.

"Did he give you your baby bottle?" Rolf asked.

"No," Eugene said, breathing funny. "He gave me my pills."

"You do drugs?" Nick asked, giggling.

"They're for asthma," Eugene explained, climbing into bed. "I can't help it."

Mr. Star strolled in, plucked the apple core from my hand, and said, "The creatures of the night might smell this delicacy and decide to attack. I'll drop it in the garbage for you." Then he turned to Eugene. "How're you doing, friend?"

"Fine," Eugene said, rasping. As he turned in bed, I could see that under the Camp Trotter blanket there was another one. It was blue with bunnies.

He *is* a baby, I thought. Rolf's right. That kid really is a baby. Baby Eugene, I said to myself. Baby, baby Eugene. I've got stuff to worry about, is all, and that's why I'm feeling so bad. But this kid is a total loss.

Mr. Star pressed the switch and it was dark again, but not too dark. The hall lights stayed on and we could see in the dim. We threw the glow-in-the-dark Frisbee back and forth between Nick and me and Rolf. Eugene even flung it a couple of times when we let him. But then Mrs. Bosco barged in and took it away.

"Boys, boys, boys, it's bedtime, bedtime, bed-time," she boomed, more like a cannon than a lullaby. And baby Eugene probably needs a lull-aby, I thought, laughing to myself.

In the dark we talked about lots of stuff. About the storm, about the monkey's paw, about Mr. Star and Miss Ivanovitch getting married. Eugene and Rolf were surprised, but they liked the idea. Eugene was even laughing about how Molly Bosco was silly, thinking Mr. Star would *ever* marry her. That's when we heard the strange noise, a kind of buzzing near the floor. I stuck my head over the side and saw Rolf, lying on his back with his mouth open, really chuffing out the snores. It's a wonder he wasn't waking himself up. We took turns shouting at him, thinking that would put a stop to it, but he snored on, turning over on his side and pulling his knees up to his chest.

Eugene took a flashlight from under his bed and turned it on Rolf's bunk. Rolf never had tucked his sheets and blanket in. It looked like he was sleeping in a clothes dryer.

"He's out," Eugene said. "Boy, I wish I could get to sleep that fast."

"You're lucky you didn't tonight," Nick told him, flicking his flashlight on. "I decided that tonight we'd truck the first guy who went to sleep."

"Truck? What's truck?" Eugene asked, laughing nervously.

"You haven't been to camp, have you?" Nick said. I didn't know what trucking was either, but I didn't say so.

"What you do is this," Nick explained. "Eugene, you grab your pillow." Eugene grabbed. The top of his baby blanket hung over the edge of his bed.

"Hobie and I'll get our flashlights out and what we do is this: Eugene, you hit Rolf over the head with your pillow. Hobie and I will stand about two feet apart and we'll shine our flashlights at Rolf and then we'll all yell, 'Truck! Truck! Watch out for the truck!' so when he wakes up he'll think our flashlights are headlights coming straight at him."

"And he'll have a heart attack," Eugene laughed.

"Somebody did it to me last summer," Nick said, "and I'm still alive."

"Did it scare you?" I asked.

"Yeah," he said, "spitless."

Somebody was walking down the hall in shoes, which meant it was an adult type, still dressed and checking. We lay still for a few minutes until there were no more hall sounds. There was only Rolf, ripping the air with his snores.

"He deserves it, you know, for keeping us awake," Eugene said, climbing out of bed with his pillow.

I got my flashlight. Nick got his, and we started on tiptoe, shoulder to shoulder, flashlight, even, walking straight from the door toward Rolf. We were a huge semi tooling down the highway at ninety miles an hour.

"Now!" Nick called.

"Honk!" Eugene shouted, pounding Rolf with his pillow, really smashing him one.

"Truck!" Nick yelled, and we drove straight at Rolf.

"Truck! It's coming straight at you," I shouted. "Truck!"

Rolf stopped snoring, sat up in bed, and stuck his arms out like he was trying to stop whatever was going to crash into him. Ducking, he rolled out of bed and onto the floor.

We laughed like crazy, Eugene most of all.

Mr. Star stuck his head in the doorway. "I've had just about enough of this foolishness. We can hear you clear at the other end of the hall."

"Sorry," we all mumbled, all but Rolf.

Rolf was foaming.

"You hit me," he told Eugene when Mr. Star had left. "I felt you hit me."

"It was just a pillow," Eugene said, crawling back into bed, still laughing. "It couldn't have hurt."

Rolf stood up and walked over to Eugene. "Don't you dare laugh at me, Eugene Kim. Don't you dare." He didn't say it loud enough for Mr. Star to hear, just low and mean. "You may have scared me out of my sleep, but at least I don't go around scared *all* the time, afraid to leave my mommy and my daddy. And I didn't need a huggy-poo from Miss Hutter when the mean, bad, old lightning flashed. And," he said, leaning over and giving a sharp yank, "I didn't have to bring a baby blanket from home to suck my thumb with." He waved the blanket over his head to make Eugene reach up for it.

"It helps me sleep," Eugene said softly.

Rolf didn't seem mad at Nick and me, even though we were the truck that almost smashed him.

"I think I'm going to sue you," he said to Eugene. "Like at school. Only I'll sue you for waking me up."

"I wasn't the only one."

"Maybe, but you *hit* me and I didn't do anything to you. You're just the baby who wants his baby blanket." He threw the blanket to me and I held it. It was soft and smelled sour.

"You admitted you did it, so you're guilty," Rolf went on. "And you aren't even sorry, because you were laughing."

"The one who sues you can't be the judge," Eugene told him. And we knew from school that was true.

"In this court he can," Rolf said.

"It was just a joke," I explained to Rolf. "It's something called trucking. You were supposed to be scared silly, that's all."

"It wasn't funny. He hurt my head." He turned back to Eugene in his bunk. "You are guilty and I fine you—"

"I didn't bring any money with me," Eugene said, eyeing his blanket and breathing again with a wheeze. "They said not to."

"OK. No money. Nick, got any ideas for a punishment?" Rolf asked, laughing suddenly, as though this was really just a big joke. "You got something to scare *him* silly?"

"Sure," Nick said, laughing with him. I think we were both glad Rolf wasn't going to lash out at us too. "Make him go up and steal a teddy bear from the girls' floor and sleep with that tonight instead of his blankie."

I didn't say anything. I guess I could have, but I didn't.

Rolf put on his official judge's voice and said, "I find you, Eugene, guilty of waking me up by hitting me when I hadn't done anything to you. Your punishment is to go get some dumb toy from the girls' floor."

Eugene started to say something, but Rolf went on. "If you don't, we'll take your baby blue blanket to breakfast tomorrow and pass it around to show everybody the bunnies."

"Give it to me," Eugene begged.

"When you come back," I told him. "After you've done it, you won't be afraid anymore."

Maybe he believed me, because he crawled out of his bed and left the room.

"I bet," Nick said, "he's on his way to tell Mr. Star on us."

"You think so?" Rolf asked. "That would be a rotten thing to do."

We walked to the door quietly, all three of us, and looked down the lighted hall, but Eugene wasn't anywhere. In the room next to ours we could hear Mrs. Bosco rumble like small thunder.

"She's *snoring!*" Rolf whispered, giggling. "How gross!"

Nick and I looked at each other and laughed. Rolf didn't even know he'd been snoring too.

"I tell you what. Let's *truck* her," Rolf whispered, and we all laughed without making a noise.

We went back into the room though, and waited.

"Maybe he ran away or something," I said

after a few minutes. "Maybe we were too mean."

"*Mean?* What'd you mean, *mean?*" Rolf laughed. "You're the one who told him it'd be good for him. We're just building his character, right?"

I picked the blue blanket off my bunk and folded it over Eugene's pillow. Then I climbed up and sat cross-legged on my bed.

When he finally ran in, Eugene was heaving like he'd been swimming a mile. He hadn't been telling on us or running away, though. In his hand was a gray stuffed kitten with a red bow around its neck. He flung it at Rolf.

"Here," he said. "*You* sleep with it."

Climbing into bed, he turned his head to the wall. I looked over the edge of my bed, but I couldn't tell if he was crying or just mad. Nobody was laughing.

I got up and went to the bathroom, because I'd forgotten to before when I tried to call home. As I was washing my hands, I looked up and saw a printed sign I hadn't noticed there before. It said "The Most Dangerous Animal in the World." The sign was over a mirror. And in th mirror was me.

1

Crocs in the Grass, Alas

"SYRUP! Hopper, more maple syrup!" R.X. demanded, like he was master and I was slave. He stuffed half a slice of bread into his mouth and passed the pitcher back. Sure enough, it was empty. French toast floated in pools of syrup on plates all around the table, but at least two kids hadn't gotten any yet.

"People, you are wasting food. I don't like it one bit," Miss Hutter said sternly. "And I want to see you cutting your food into smaller pieces." R.X. looked up at the ceiling. Would she let me dip my french fries in catsup if I went to that lunch I'd won? Fat chance. Maybe I could wiggle out my back tooth just at noon on Thursday, and suffer too much to go.

Everybody was quiet, looking down at our

French toast islands. But the pitcher did have only a spoonful left in it, so I tilted my white chef's cap on my head and went to the kitchen for more.

After breakfast was over and I'd scraped all the sticky plates and taken the last sweep with the sponge, I went outside with Molly, who'd been hopper at the next table. It was sunny, and so warm we didn't even need jackets. We inspected an oak tree next to the front steps. It had a white slit down the side where lightning had torn the bark away.

"Who won your scavenger hunt last night?" Molly asked as we hurried back to the lodge. Inspection was in fifteen minutes and I hadn't made my bed.

"Scavenger hunt?" I asked.

"You know," Molly said impatiently, "the one I gave Eugene my gray cat for. Who won it?"

"Oh, *that* scavenger hunt." Eugene, you fox, I thought. That wasn't bad at all. I'd wondered why a posse hadn't come cat hunting. "Eugene won," I told her. "He won because of your cat, but Rolf slept with it, so you'll have to get it back from him."

"You're *kidding!*" she said. Then she shrugged her shoulders. "I don't care if Rolf likes me or not. He's not cueshee. We thought the rest of you would be coming, you know, looking for more cats. And we waited for you. Actually," she said

90

as we got to the lodge, "we were waiting on both sides of our door with pillows ready to smash you over the head. But we laughed so much that when we whammed our four pillows at the first guy who walked through the door, it was Miss Ivanovitch checking on the noise. She got such a blast it probably made her even shorter." Molly giggled.

"What'd she do?"

"She said if we weren't quiet, she was going to drag her mattress into our room and camp out on the floor. So we shut up and went to sleep. That would have been pure poison."

Our room did not win inspection. We didn't even come close. Mr. Star stood with his arms crossed while Rolf stuffed his pajamas into a drawer and tucked in his sheets, sort of. And when Mr. Star pulled Molly's red-bowed cat from under Rolf's bunk, nobody claimed it.

Mrs. Bosco yodeled, and we gathered on the front porch in our four sections. Miss I. explained that what her group was going to do first was called the log jam, which sounded pretty weird. We followed her up the hill, through the woods, and into a clearing, where there was a genuine log on the ground.

"OK, Tape," she said. "All aboard." It wasn't a very thick log—only about a foot across— though it was so long it could have held at least twenty kids. We climbed on it and stood there like thirteen bumps.

"One thing about being human," Miss Ivanovitch said, "is that you can think. It isn't just instinct that makes us tick. This is a kind of puzzle to see if you can get yourself out of a mess by using your heads." The thirteen of us teetered on the log.

"The mess you're in now," she explained, "is that on all sides of that log you're on there is quicksand, and if you step off the log, the quicksand will suck you under. Got that?"

I looked down at the solid ground and imagined it was something oozy, like oatmeal.

"This is creepy," Lisa said.

"So, here is the puzzle." She pointed with a stick to a place between Molly and Eugene, roughly in the middle of the log. "The six of you on one side of this middle line have to exchange places with the seven on the other side without falling off into the mire."

We stood there for a minute, rocking.

"Is this a trick question?" Molly asked.

"If we were grasshoppers, no problem," Marshall said.

"It's not possible."

"How do we do it?" Eugene asked her.

"That's the question," Miss Ivanovitch said.

People started talking all at once, with nobody listening. And no matter what we tried, we fell off. If that quicksand had been a little oozier, we'd all have been sucked into the center of the earth. "Let's do something fun," Cindy from 4A moaned.

"It can't be done," I said.

"Of course it can. But you're going to have to help each other, instead of fighting. You may even have to touch each other," Miss Ivanovitch explained.

"Me, touch *her?*" Nick said, poking Cindy in the ribs. She jumped to the front, yelled, "Cooties!" and poked him back. He fell into the quicksand. It was useless.

"I know!" Lisa said. "I've got an idea. One half kind of squats down, like—"

"I've got a better idea," Molly yelled. "All we've got to do—"

"But if we—"

"Listen to Lisa," Marshall said.

"I have an *idea,*" she began again.

"Then *say* it," Molly told her impatiently.

"OK," Lisa began for the millionth time, "my team, spread out so there's, like, a foot or so between each person. And then squat down very low. The other team can just step over us . . . sort of like leapfrog."

"Then we'll have changed sides. She's right, you know," Marshall said.

A few of us fell off anyway, but it worked better than anything else we'd tried. So we collapsed on the ground that was no longer quicksand.

"Was it the right answer?" Lisa asked.

"It worked," Miss Ivanovitch told her. "Congratulations, Lisa," and Lisa beamed.

"That was easy," Molly said. "Let's do something else."

We did a whole batch of People Puzzles. In one we had to crawl through triangles of rope that were supposed to be electric fences. We ran through a maze of tires and climbed over a slippery log that was lashed about six feet off the ground between two trees. That wasn't any piece of cake. I was dangling with my head and arms over the log, desperate for help, when Nick yelled up, "It's OK, Hanson. If you fall, I've got this great little graveyard for you." Marshall, who was sitting up on the log, grabbed me by the belt and pulled me over safe.

The last puzzle we did was using two planks to get all of us across five tree stumps. Molly kept trying to boss us, but her ideas didn't always work. So, when Aretha said, "We've got to cooperate, you guys," Molly asked her if *Sesame Street* was her very *very* favorite show. Aretha was right, though. It never worked when we were arguing.

"Watch out!" Miss Ivanovitch yelled whenever we stumbled. "There are crocs in the grass, alas." By the time we were through, we'd each had at least one toe bitten off by the crocodiles who were supposed to be starving underneath the tree stumps. We were tired, too.

"You're clever," Miss Ivanovitch said. "No doubt about that. I'll keep that in mind. Now, if you can make it with all your wounds, we're going to capture some small creatures and have a race." And she started off in the direction of the lodge.

"We may be smart," I said to the Tapes I was walking with, "but there's something in the boy's john . . ." Everybody laughed. "No, really. There's this sign in there above the mirror."

"There's a sign in the girls' bathroom, too," Lisa told me. " 'The Most Dangerous Animal in the World'."

"What's so dangerous about me?" I asked, though I was afraid I knew. "I mean, the animals out here are always eating each other up."

"Don't be silly. That's a joke mirror," Molly said.

"No, it's not," Eugene told her.

Miss Ivanovitch told us to hunt animals on the way back and put them in little screened boxes she'd brought along. As we searched Miss I. called, "Don't hurt them, my dears. When we're finished, we'll free them so they can tend to their business." I thought about my picture in the mirror and didn't catch anything.

"It's like a scavenger hunt, don't you think, Eugene?" I said.

His eyes turned suspicious. "Who told you?"

The two of us shook a bush and woke a bee, which we did not follow.

95

"Molly," I said, smiling brightly. "And I think that was very very very clever. I wouldn't have thought of it myself."

He did not smile back.

Nobody caught a fox and put it in a box, or an armadillo or a camel, either. We did get a cricket, a centipede, a big black ant, and, even, down by the marsh, a small frog. Aretha soaked her sneakers bagging him.

We took our animals to an open spot, drew a big circle in the dirt, put them in the middle, and watched to see which would get out of the circle first. I thought it would be the frog easy, because it was the biggest. So did most people. But it wasn't. The frog just sat there.

"He's scared stiff," Nick said.

The cricket jumped back and forth, getting nowhere.

"He's scared silly," Eugene laughed, and the three of us from room nine smiled at each other.

The centipede ambled along. But the big black ant made it out in less than a minute. He didn't even wait for his trophy.

Down on the Farm

"Come on, it won't hurt you. Who'll hold it? How about you, little girl?" Lunch was over. We'd finished planning skits for the night's fireside program, and we Tapes were back to nature again, learning about bird banding.

Molly backed off. Either she didn't want to be called "little girl" or she was afraid to hold a pecky little yellow warbler.

The Camp Trotter guide man had just taken the warbler out of a metal mesh cage that had seeds in it. Sometime during the morning the dumb bird had just hopped right in and gotten caught. The Camp Trotter man meant to snap a metal band around its leg, giving the bird a number for identification, but the bird already had a band. "This is

97

one of last year's," he said, and he handed the bird to me without asking if I wanted it.

Everybody stared as I took it. There was no way to say no. He started talking about migration and stuff, but I couldn't follow what he said because I had this wild bird cupped in my hands.

It pecked at my thumbs like needle pricks when you're getting a splinter out. Its claws scratched at my little fingers, and its heart beat as fast as a purr against my palms. My heart beat fast, too. He wanted to go home. So did I.

"Can I let him go?" I asked, interrupting.

"Anybody else want a turn?" He looked around. Nobody else did.

"Hold fast," Miss Ivanovitch called. "I remembered my camera this afternoon." She took a picture of me and the bird, neither one of us looking happy. And then I let it fly away home.

After the bird banding place, we hiked to the farm. Miss Ivanovitch lined us up in front of its old white house and took our pictures all together. Then she snapped kids sitting in the old claw-foot bathtub filled with hay in the barnyard. Kids grabbed hay and stuck it in other kids' shirts and into their hair, great fistfuls of it, wanting pictures of that, too.

"Don't play with their food," she called. And she snapped the lens cap back on the camera.

A baby goat wandered up and nuzzled her leg. "Oh, look, do," she said, "it's the new kid in town."

"Miss Ivanovitch, that's *terrible*," Aretha told her, giggling. The little kid sprang forward, *ka-pong, ka-pong,* and two bigger goats chased after it. So did Vince from 4A.

Inside the barn, chickens sat on nests. I'd never seen a chicken on a nest before.

"Are there any eggs?" Miss Ivanovitch asked.

"I don't see any," Marshall told her, holding his hands behind his back as he looked.

"Reach under the hens and check."

"You're kidding," Molly said, taking a step away. The hens' heads shifted toward her. "They'll attack."

Eugene marched right up to the nest, stuck his hand under the hen, and brought out an egg. "Like magic," he said, holding it up with two fingers.

"Why is it brown?" Lisa asked. "That's, like, gross."

"Because it's a brown egg," he told her.

"Real eggs are white," she said. Like, *I* never saw a brown egg before, and I've been eating eggs all my life. The eggs in the grocery store are white." She looked at it closely, her nose wrinkled. "Is it safe to eat?" she asked Miss Ivanovitch.

"Some are just brown and some are white. It depends on the chicken," Eugene went on. "Chicken eggs are chicken eggs. My grandparents have a farm, and that's how I know." He reached under another hen and brought out one more brown egg. If Eugene could do that without flinching, why did he need a baby blanket? It didn't make sense.

A black-and-white cat tunneled from under the barn. Vince and I both chased it, but I swooped it up. "I found an owl," I called to Nick, and everybody else thought I was bonkers. It was the same hard-purring cat I'd carried to the lodge the day before.

From the farm we could see the cemetery, only a city block or so away. But we didn't have paper with us. Besides, there was no way to sneak over. Miss Ivanovitch was thinking about the cemetery, too.

"I wonder if I could break away for a couple of minutes and make a fast rubbing?" she said, almost to herself. She fingered a roll of paper in the big bag she carried over her shoulder, chewed on her lip, and then looked at her watch. She sighed and said, "It's three o'clock, my dears, and we're supposed to be in those orange pontoon boats ready to measure the depth of lovely Lake Lindaloma at three-ten."

A goat who wanted its picture taken before we left began to nibble on her camera.

"OK, put the rabbits back in their hutches. We've got to leave."

"This rabbit is totally like velvet," Aretha told her. "Pet it."

Vince, chasing after a rabbit he'd put down to

see if it would hop, slipped in a slick of mud and fell flat.

"Oh, my dear, you look as though you could grow a crop of corn on those jeans alone," Miss Ivanovitch said as she scraped him off with a stick and splashed him with water from the pump.

Molly stuck a brown egg under the flow of water. "Can I take this back with me?" she asked.

"I hesitate to ask what you'd *do* with an egg, Molly, but the answer, in any case, is no. It belongs on the farm. It may even have had plans to be a baby chick."

Finally she checked to see that everything was in place, locked up, and then announced, "To the boats! We're going to take the temperature of the lake and test it for bacteria. So, if you fall in, we'll know how deep you'll sink, how cold you'll be, and what's alive in there with you."

We looked like scarecrows, hay sticking out of our pockets and shirts. And as we marched, Miss Ivanovitch told us that we were off to see the Wizard of the Docks, who was going to tell us all about Algae in Wonderland.

"See," Aretha whispered to Molly. "She's even funny like Mr. Star when you give her a chance."

Molly rolled her eyes. "A laugh riot," she said.

By suppertime we were tired and hungry. Even kids who didn't like meatloaf loaded it with catsup and ate. Though they had been quiet most of the day, my woollyworms had an appetite too. Besides, meatloaf is one of my favorites.

After supper, Nick conned two sheets of drawing paper and a couple of crayons out of Ms. O'Malley, telling her we had this art project we needed to work on. But by the time we'd played another kickball game and seen a film on bats in the recreation room, I was zonked out. I was ready to draw a lake, a couple of trees, and a cat, give that to Miss Ivanovitch, and call it quits.

"The fire is going strong," Miss Ivanovitch called when the movie was over, and I looked out the window, half expecting to see Smokey the Bear shaking his finger at her.

"Oh, my, a campfire, that's glorious," Mrs. Bosco announced, pulling herself up from the flowered sofa. "Shall I tell another fireside story? I have a treasury of them."

"Not tonight," Miss Hutter said, a little too fast and a little too loud. "Last night was charming," she added, "and we thank you very much, of course, but tonight we have Silence, Skits, and Singing."

Here, Kitty, Kitty

SILENCE came first. Except for some tripping and burping, we walked in total, mysterious quiet through the woods and up a hill into a clearing. The fire wasn't there. They had us all lie down in a circle, our feet toward the middle, so we could stare up at the millions of stars. The moon looked like a canoe.

First we searched for star pictures, but I never do see bears up there or Hercules or the three parts of anybody's belt. The Big Dipper, that's easy. But that's all.

Then they told us to lie still with our eyes closed and listen to the sounds of the night. It's true that with your eyes closed you hear better. Somehow, you'd think that so far from the city and shopping centers and cars and all it would be quiet, but it wasn't. *We* were quiet for once, but the crickets rubbed their legs nonstop, and the trees made a racket when the wind blew through them. Chains clinked where the boats were tied down at the pier, a plane flew over, and a dog barked far away.

After we'd listened to night noises for a while, Mr. Star said he was going to call an owl and see if one would answer. Lying on the ground with us, one of the spokes of our wheel, he told us how owls are predators and what they eat. Big owls sometimes catch skunks, he said. Owls don't even care if they get sprayed with the stink, because they've got a lousy sense of smell. Small owls swallow mice and birds and snails whole, he said, and after they eat, they spit out pellets of all the leftover fur and bones and feathers. Everybody went "Yuck." He waited a little and then went "Woo-woo," kind of soft like a pigeon.

Nothing answered, except the leaves and the crickets and the clinking chains.

"Wooooo," he went again.

I shivered. What if this huge owl swooped down, picked up the smallest kid in the ring—Tracey probably—laid her pellet on us and flew away without a noise? Mr. Star had said their wings were soundless.

"Woooo-oooo," Mr. Star tried again. He was just two down from me and I knew it was still him calling, but I heard kids say, "I heard one answer, did you?"

Mr. Star *woo*-ed once more, and after awhile cleared his throat and said, "Some owls hoot, some laugh, some shriek." I think he was giving us a lecture to make up for the bird's not answering him. "Some owls snore," he went on. That broke everybody up. Owls snoring. The only owl that was going to answer us was a laughing owl.

"I know how to call birds," Nick said, turning his head to me.

"Sure. Sure you do," I told him.

"I *do*. It's easy." He raised his voice. "Here, bird! Here, bird!" And from somewhere near in the woods, a bird answered, "Wooooooo-wooooooo."

We couldn't stay flat any longer. Everybody was eyes open and whistling like you do for a dog and calling, "Here, birdie! Here, owl!" and the silence was gone for good.

Next came Singing. We walked to the campfire mumbling this song we'd learned in music class before we left school. It was about "jolly flames a-dancing" and "pale moonlight entrancing."

Miss Ivanovitch had been in charge of making the fire and it was a knockout, shaped like a teepee and spitting sparks up like crazy. Sitting-logs were set in a big ring around the fire. Kids kept shifting around on them until they got Mr. S. and Miss I. next to each other, because by then everybody knew for sure they were practically engaged.

The fire felt warm on our faces, and we were all

sitting there smelling the wood burn. When Mr. Plate stood up and raised his hand, we were already almost quiet. Mr. Plate was in charge of the program he called Fireside Fun.

"First, we're going to play a warm-up game," he announced, "called Telephone. What I'll do is whisper a sentence to the two people on each side of me and we'll hear how it changes. That way you can see how well you've learned to listen." A few people groaned. Telephone is a second-grade game. But since he was just a student teacher, Mr. Plate might not have known.

He started out the same thing going opposite directions around the circle and after it had gotten whispered one way through twenty some ears, it came out, "A glove ate more thread than my damp daughter." Mr. Plate said that wasn't right. At the other end, Vince said it was "I shove trout ashore dead and they're hotter." Mr. Plate hadn't started with that either, it turned out. He'd said (gag), "I love Outdoor Ed at Camp Trotter." It was better our way.

Then it was skit time. Each group had worked one out. The Lindalomas all got up and sang "Great Green Gobs of Greasy Grimy Gopher Guts." The Bowls did a skit about a barber shop I never did understand, but it had a lot of screaming and catsup in it. The CIA wound kids up in rolls of toilet paper they called Do-It-Yourself-Mummy kits.

The Scotch Tape did Fortune Teller. It was

Molly's idea, so she got to be Swami. She sat crosslegged, a towel draping her head and a sheet twined around her like a cape. She faced the campfire and swayed back and forth, asking the Spirit of the Great Outdoors to help her read fortunes.

She read fortunes from shoes. Each of the rest of the Tape brought her a shoe to read. She turned the first one over carefully, stared at its bottom, and said in her high, flutey voice, "You have a beautiful soul." Kids groaned, but she went on. "And you will go on TV or be in other fancy shoe business." The groans got louder. The shoe belonged to R.X., who tap dances. Molly flicked it over her shoulder, and R.X. ran to pick it up before somebody else could.

Over a pair of somebody's high-toppers she shrieked, "You're *so* high-strung!" Then she tossed that shoe behind her, crying, "Let yourself go!"

I brought her one of Michelle's Adidas that had tears along both sides where mud had leaked in. She held her nose with one hand and threw the shoe far away with the other, saying, "You don't give a hoot. You pollute!" Michelle jumped up high to catch the shoe, because Molly had tossed it as far as it was stinky. Somebody else caught it and, while Michelle chased after, the shoe got flung from kid to kid like it was a long-dead toad.

Then Lisa brought one of Miss Ivanovitch's heavy, worn hiking boots up. She bowed as she

presented it. The corners of Molly's mouth twitched. She closed her eyes, held the boot up high over her head in both hands, and said, "This belongs to someone who is going on a long, long trip." She grabbed it by the laces, swung it around in circles, and let it fly. The trip, I guess, was supposed to be to the moon. And, while it didn't orbit, nobody saw where it fell short.

"Next," Molly demanded, holding her hands in front of her like she was in a trance.

"Molly," Miss Hutter said, sharply. "You have thrown the shoe into the bushes. It belongs to Miss Ivanovitch. We must find it at once."

Molly shook her head like she was trying to wake up. "Oh, my," she said, "I'm so sorry. I didn't do it on purpose. Which way did it go?"

Kids started getting up and moving out in all directions. Nobody was sure which way it had gone.

"I'm afraid it's too dark to look now," Miss Ivanovitch said. "Tomorrow morning will do. It's all right, Molly. You were just too involved in the skit. I expect you'd be a terrific actress."

Molly smiled. That's what she thought too.

Mr. Plate got everybody standing, even though our skit wasn't really over, and we stood there with a lot more sneakers in our hands. "OK, now, everybody, we'll sing 'Day is Done,' " he said, "because it is." He sounded glad. "Everybody hold hands to sing." Nobody did. "OK, now, everybody hold hands so we can be one big circle, one group, one family." We held, but there was a lot of grumbling, oosicking, and cootie-shooting. As we sang, we watched to see if Mr. Star would hold Miss Ivanovitch's hand, too. He did. It was like happily ever after.

Miss Ivanovitch was standing on one foot, and, after we finished singing "safely rest" at the end, Mr. Star helped her down the path. Nick winked at me.

On the way back, Nick and I talked about the night and whether we should go out in it. The moon wasn't even half there, but our own flashlights were still bright.

"Listen," Nick whispered, "we hit the sack right away and pretend to be asleep. Then we sneak out as soon as Mr. Star has made his bed check."

I yawned and stretched.

"You want to chicken out?" he asked.

I wanted to.

"Listen, you tore that rubbing as much as I did," he said. And that was a fact.

"You guys," Rolf whispered as we walked in the room, "let's stay up really late and raid somebody." He had plans, too. "Maybe we could cruise around and do a little trucking."

Eugene was already in bed. "If you truck me tonight," he told us, "I will let the air out of your tires and make you crash." He flashed his light in all three of our eyes. It wasn't fair. Eugene didn't look homesick any more. But the night still grabbed at my throat, making it hard for me to swallow. I needed at least to call home and check, but I couldn't let Nick see me doing it.

We both yawned big and took our shoes off. I grabbed one of Nick's and yelled in a high voice, "Oh, your tongue looks furry. It's probably fatal." Nick crossed his eyes and collapsed on the floor.

When Rolf left the room, we crawled into bed with our clothes on and turned to the wall so he wouldn't see if our eyes flickered. Then we waited.

Down the hall I could hear kids calling, "I am not!" "Give that back!" "My nose is bleeding."

After lights out, Nick started fake snoring, and if I hadn't known what he was doing, I'd have thrown a pillow at him. Rolf complained to Eugene about how we weren't having any fun at all, but soon he was snoring, too, for real. I lay there close to the ceiling listening to the crickets outside, wishing it was tomorrow and the bus had just pulled in at school and both my folks were there meeting me with a batch of chocolate chip cookies and telling me how great it was to be the three of us again. And telling me, too, how the firemen had rescued Fido from the top of a TV antenna and how the FBI had found my bike painted gold in a raid on an international bike ring, and how . . . I decided when Nick got to sleep really, I would get up and call home. The crickets chirped on and on.

111

"But," I was asking this lady dressed in blue, "but aren't you going to . . . But I thought you fought . . ." And the lady was about to say something very, very important to me when suddenly, "Hobie," somebody hissed in my ear. "Hobie, come on!" A hand was shaking my shoulder.

"Who . . ." I asked. "Wha . . . time?"

"We fell asleep," Nick was telling me. "It's eleven thirty-two. My watch says. Come on. Carry your shoes till we get outside, and don't forget your flashlight. I've got the paper and crayon. We ought to be able to do it in an hour."

Rubbing my eyes and shaking the sleep out, I climbed down from the bunk as quietly as I could. We tiptoed through the dimly lighted hall past Mrs. Bosco's room. She was rumbling in her sleep like a cement mixer.

The front door clicked when we opened it, but nobody appeared, so we sat down on the outside steps to put on our sneakers. The crickets weren't asleep yet, but the night was quieter and the air cooler than it had been during Silence and Skits.

All we had to do was follow the road to the graveyard. Looking behind and in front both, we watched for cars and ghosts and teachers. As we jogged, I could feel things alive and watching from both sides of the road, but no one real knew we were there. If we got trucked in the deep, dark night, nobody would know.

By the time we reached the cemetery, I felt like I'd been running a hundred miles, a hundred thousand miles, with some mysterious predator chasing after. Something shaped like a shadow.

Nick, though, was all excited. Every step and he loved it more.

"Don't you feel like you're skipping school and nobody's ever going to find out? This is so excellent," he said as we reached the graveyard.

"I'm tired," I told him, and that's all I could say about how I felt. He'd have rolled on the graves laughing at the rest. He was scareproof.

As we searched our way down the main path of the cemetery, we heard a car coming on the highway. Flicking our lights off, we fell flat. The dead were quiet in the night. Not even a breeze moved. The car slowed down, but kept going. When everything was totally black again, we got up. Nick turned on his light and located the baby with wings. We took turns rubbing and holding the paper and the light. It was better to be the one rubbing because then you had something to do. I held the paper last, watching for cars and trying not to stare at the tombstones where things seemed to shift in the shadows.

"Can't you hurry?" I asked Nick. "My fingers are numb."

"Finished!" he said. "One more sweep and I'm finished." He leaned into it.

After the last stroke we sat on the grass away from the mounds and looked at what we'd done.

113

It was excellent. Except that the paper had been moved a very little bit and the angel had a moustache because of it, the rubbing was practically perfect. True, Nick hadn't checked the color of the crayon and we'd done it in purple instead

Luella Winston
Died April 4, 1858
3 Weeks, 4 Days old

of black, but it was still excellent. I began to feel good for the first time since he woke me. Rolling the rubbing up into a tube, I looked up at the stars through it and then tucked it under my arm.

On the way back we headed down the middle of the highway like it was the yellow brick road, figuring *everybody* was asleep by twelve-thirteen, the time it said on Nick's digital watch. We swung our flashlights dark by our sides, though, just in case.

"Hey, Hobie, look, it's our old friend," Nick shouted, pointing ahead at the side of the road. "Here, kitty, kitty," he called, running ahead. "Here, owl!" The creature moved toward us slowly as we galloped his way, calling and whistling. And I bet we were only ten feet away before I saw that, while he *was* black and white, he wasn't our cat. This kitty was big and black and furry with white stripes down both sides and had eyes like tiny red marbles. He was a skunk.

Squirt

I grabbed Nick by the arm. "Back up slow or he'll shoot!" I said, my voice squeaking. I pulled at Nick again, but he didn't move. The skunk eyed us to see, maybe, if we were his friends. I tried a smile, but my mouth wouldn't work.

"Hurry," I hissed at Nick, yanking his arm. But he was like a stone statue. "Please, Nick." I never knew what it meant before, scared stiff, but that's what Nick was.

The skunk wasn't scared. He was mad. He stamped his front feet on the pavement and began a low half purr, half growl. Then he lifted his tail high, the white tip hanging limp like a flag in no wind. I knew what was going to happen next. I knew because Mr. Star had told us in class. The skunk was going to turn around, raise that tip, and squirt us straight from jets in his bottom with an oily yellow stink. Everybody had practically rolled on the floor laughing when he told us in school what fantastic backward aim the skunk has.

"Truck!" I gasped in Nick's ear, thinking that might move him. "Truck!" When it didn't, I grabbed his belt and pulled. Mr. Star had said if the smell got on your clothes, you soaked them in ammonia for a week, buried them in the ground for a week, and then threw them away. He didn't say what you did with the people inside.

The skunk arched his back and hissed again.

Like I was Superman, I dragged Nick down the road toward the graveyard. I don't know how I got so strong. But when I couldn't go any farther, I rolled us off into the ditch and grabbed my nose. Nick sucked in his breath. I think he'd been holding it all that time. "It . . . never . . . knees . . . locked," he gasped.

As we lay hiding, listening to our hearts bump and our breath heave, I realized that the air I was gulping tasted like ditch dirt and nothing worse. Letting go of my nose, I found out it was true. The skunk hadn't sprayed—yet.

"Whoooo," I heard, somewhere in the distance. "Whooo." Owls, I remembered, eat skunks. Owl is predator. Skunk is prey.

"Whoooo," I answered low. "Woooooo." The

owl, what if that owl hears me, swoops over, snatches the skunk up for a midnight snack, and carries him away in the sky? What if?

"You crazy?" Nick whispered, no longer speechless. "Now he'll find us sure." We listened and heard nothing. No skunk, no owl. "Maybe he's gone. Can you see?"

Slowly I raised my head out of the ditch and looked. At first everything was fuzzy and dark, then about thirty feet away, maybe, I saw the skunk. And the skunk saw me. I was certain of it. Maybe it *was* the "whooo's" or maybe he just smelled us, but he knew for sure where we were. And he was heading straight at us down our yellow brick road.

I was just sinking back down in a panic when I turned my head to look again. The skunk wasn't alone. I blinked my eyes to see clearer. Coming over the top of the hill behind, a flashlight beam swept the road and the ditch.

"*Ho-bie! Ni-ick!*" a voice called. I couldn't see who had the flashlight, but I knew we'd been found out.

"*Hobie! Nick!* Where are you?" the voice cried. Steaming down the highway, gaining on our skunk, was Miss Ivanovitch. When she stopped yelling, I called back. I had to.

"Skunk!" I sang out quietly, hoping she would hear and the skunk couldn't. "Skunk!" He better not understand English, I thought, and think I'm

118

calling him to come. "Skunk!" Please, Miss Ivanovitch, I wished, closing my eyes tight, please don't rush up to pet the kitty.

I waited as long as I could stand it. Then, lifting my head again, just eye-level over the ditch, I tried to see what was happening.

Her flashlight still glowed and the skunk marched on—our way. Nick lay face down on his arm, breathing hard. Hiding my head again, I looked up at the stars, quadrillions of them, *too* many to wish on, but I wished anyway. I am asleep and this is some weird dream, I decided. Or a nightmare, maybe, galloping out of control. That girl Dorothy in *The Wizard of Oz,* all she had to do was say "There's no place like home," and she got there. There's no place like home, I thought as hard as I could, clenching my fists, There's no place like home. But I could hear paws on the pavement now, and the dirt was not my bed.

"He's coming," I barely breathed aloud. "Freeze."

"Last time, you said run," Nick sobbed.

The paw steps clicked closer and closer until I could hear breathing, too. It is the year, I thought, of the stink. Forever after they are going to remember this Outdoor Ed as the Big Stink. The whole place will reek of us unless they soak us in ammonia and bury us for a week. The footsteps stopped, but the breathing didn't.

At the edge of the ditch, the pointy-faced skunk was peering at me. I did not close my eyes. I did not blink them, even. I did sweat. He opened his mouth and his teeth shone. He'd won the battle paws down. Maybe he was laughing. For sure he wasn't scared. All he had to do was whip around, lift his tail, and aim *rat-a-tat-tat*.

Instead, though, he stood there for a minute, staring, and then, swishing his vast bushy tail, he turned and disappeared down the road.

Even after his steps had faded, we waited five minutes—ten—a long time, listening, until all we could hear was each other breathing. Maybe he had walked a ways and then snuck back into our

ditch to surprise us from behind. My eyes were closed, my fingers crossed, and my scalp was prickling as if tiny ants were moving in with all their gear when a voice above us whispered, "You OK?"

She smelled like perfume. Miss Ivanovitch sat down on the side of the road, her feet in the ditch. That's when Nick began to cry. Actually, it was a sort of half cry, half laugh. "He's gone?" Nick asked.

"He is gone," she said. "Tail down. Saving his spray for something a little more wild than you two." She smiled. She *didn't* say, For this cute trick I'll see to it you stay in fourth grade forever.

"How did you know where we were?" I asked her.

"Well, I heard the word 'skunk' kind of floating through the air, but I didn't actually see it until one of you peered from your hiding place," she told us, "and all at once I saw skunk and prey." She looked down at Nick and shook her head. "I didn't know what to do. It's a genuine problem, I thought, no crocs in the grass, but a real live skunk on the road. I don't know when I've been so scared." She stood up and shook her shoulders like she wanted to get rid of the feeling in them.

"It worked," I told her, "doing nothing worked."

"You guys were fantastic," she said, leaning toward us. "What a disaster if you'd panicked."

"If?" Nick laughed, embarrassed.

"Come on," she said, "it's late."

"Is everybody looking for us?"

"Nobody but me. I thought I knew where you were and I *knew* it was my fault you were there. Look, I ought not to have lashed out at you yesterday. I'm sorry." She brushed her hair back and rubbed her front teeth with her fingers. "Maybe I'm not ready to be a teacher, do you think, losing my temper like that?"

Nick and I didn't say anything. No teacher had asked us a question like that.

"And maybe," she said, "I should have reported you gone."

I didn't know teachers thought about making mistakes. It was like they were always right and we were supposed to be wrong.

"Race you back," she said, smiling suddenly and starting off. She had no shoes on. She was wearing red-and-green striped socks, which was why we hadn't heard her walking up.

"How'd you know we were gone?" I asked as we started back, brushing chunks of ditch dirt off our clothes.

"Eugene," she said, trotting faster.

"How'd *he* know?" Nick asked, his voice shaking only a little now.

"Actually, he only had clues. When you left he was awake, and he heard you say something about crayon and paper and how it would take only an hour." She made a little bow as she ran and said, "I used my remarkable Sherlock Holmes handy-dandy deductions and figured out what that meant. It meant the graveyard."

"But we left our room late. It was eleven thirty-two exactly. Why did you come in at all? Were you just checking?" Nick asked her. It was

123

like a mystery, suddenly, since she was Sherlock Holmes.

"Ah, you weren't the only ones awake," she said, sighing. We walked easy now, in the dark. "Just after eleven forty-five Eugene invaded the girls' hall."

"Eugene?" Nick and I said together.

"Somebody disguised as Eugene," Nick told her. "No way he'd do that again."

"Again? No, it was Eugene. He appeared at the top of the steps carrying a gray stuffed cat with a red bow. Somebody had set Molly's clock to go off at eleven forty-five, and it clanged as loud as the fire alarm at school. The place went wild. Molly had shut the alarm off by the time Eugene came, but all the girls were standing in the hall in their pajamas and nightgowns, and the poor kid hardly knew what to do."

"What *did* he do?" Nick asked.

"Well, he threw the cat at Molly like it was a football and fled. I think he really had come to talk to me about your leaving, but the girls didn't give him a chance." She shook her head. "I don't know why he had the gray cat."

Nick and I looked at each other and laughed.

The lodge was in sight now. All the rooms were dark.

"After that," she went on, lowering her voice, "there was this terrific disturbance around midnight in the boys' hall. Marshall, R.X., and some

124

other boys had pushed their bunks together, built a fort by draping their blankets across the beds, and were telling ghost stories that ended up in pillow fights. They howled, and that woke the boys next door. And the boys next door started pounding on the walls. I was right at the top of the steps, so I came down to be stern. What a night!" She laughed.

"But *we* weren't making any noise," I said. "We weren't *there*."

"Actually," she said, "I had something to talk with you about, and I thought if all the yelling and pounding had woken you—"

"To talk with me?"

She looked over at Nick, who was flashing his light up at the stars. "It'll keep," she said.

Slowly, slowly we crept up the lodge steps and in the front door. The halls were so quiet you'd think there'd never been a pillow fight inside a blanket fort, or ghosts, or bumps in the night.

She put her finger to her lips, then waved goodbye with both hands. When Nick had turned into our room, I started back to ask what she'd wanted to tell me, but she was gone. I'd decided there was only one thing she could need to talk to me about. She must know something from home. I thought about following her to the girls' floor, but if I ran into Molly or Lisa I'd never be able to go back to school again.

"Hobie," Nick hissed down the hall, sticking

125

his head out the door. I hurried into the room. "They catch us in our clothes like this and they'll ask us questions and we've had it."

Rolf was snoring away. Eugene sat up in bed and stared at us, his eyes wide open.

"What time is it?" he asked.

"Twelve forty-five," Nick told him.

"Then it took more than an hour. I was worried," he said, "about the ghosts at midnight. And I kept thinking about deep, dark holes with hairy green hands in them. That place is creepy enough in the daylight." He leaned forward. "Did . . . did she find you?"

"Yeah," Nick said, climbing into his bunk above Rolf. He tossed a heap of dirty clothes on the floor and got under the covers wearing his underwear.

"Are you mad at me for telling?" Eugene asked him. "I knew I shouldn't have." He watched me take off my socks. "Look, I know you guys don't get scared like I do, but *anything* could have happened in the night."

"Anything did," I told him.

He looked puzzled, but shrugged it off. "Did you get a good rubbing for Miss Ivanovitch? She said she was really mad at herself for yelling at you about killing the first one."

"Yeah," I told him, yawning as I climbed into bed. "We got a really good one. We did it in purple. It's got a—" And then the panic hit me, pow, in the stomach. Nick?" I called. "Nick!" But he was breathing heavy.

"He's asleep," Eugene said, craning his neck to look. "His mouth is open."

"Nick!" I called again, anyway. "Do you have the rubbing?" But he didn't. I knew he didn't. I had carried the rubbing myself. And it was lying scrunched in a ditch somewhere down the cemetery road, ants crawling through its tunnel, waiting for a high-tailed skunk to pass by.

The
Announcement

"BEAUTIFULLY behaved! That's what I have to say, and you can quote me. Beautifully behaved. I would be a chaperone for those lovely, lovely boys any day." As they walked down to breakfast, Mrs. Bosco was shouting to the world around and Miss Hutter in particular how perfect we were. "Not a peep out of them after their nine-thirty bedtime. Not a peep. And *I* am a very light sleeper."

"Um," Miss Hutter answered. She must have been down for the midnight wall-banging.

Nick and I, walking behind them, held our knuckles to our mouths to keep from laughing. We also had our fingers holding our noses to keep from smelling. A breeze whipping in cool weather was also blowing in the strong, sharp smell of skunk. It was even worse than I had remembered. Kitty-Kitty must have met somebody he didn't like. Maybe the owl came and picked him up by the scruff of his neck. Mrs. Bosco pulled her red cowboy neckerchief up over her nose like a bandit.

"And I've kept my lip buttoned about Miss Ivanovitch," she told Miss Hutter even louder. "Even when Molly asked specially. Miss Ivanovitch was so gracious to her during that darling skit, didn't you think?"

"Um," Miss Hutter said again. I got the feeling she wasn't crazy about Mrs. Bosco, but was too polite to let her know.

"And when will the announcement be?" Mrs. Bosco asked.

"I expect she'll decide that," Miss Hutter answered as R.X., Rolf, and Marshall ran up to join us. Eugene had gone down early to be a hopper. We told them about the announcement.

"I guess the girls are right about their getting married," R.X. said, shaking his head. "But that sure was quick. Miss Ivanovitch only substituted three or four times around school after she subbed for us."

"Once you meet her you don't forget her, though," Marshall said.

Halfway down the hill, Miss Ivanovitch was walking alone. "I'll be back in a minute," I said to the guys. "There's something I want to find out."

129

"Find out if we'll be invited. I want to throw rice," Rolf called after me.

"The sheet of instructions said to bring *two* pairs of shoes," I told her as I ran up. She had only one boot on. The shirt under her painters' overalls was blue with big white dots. Today's socks were yellow-and-white.

"The sheet of instructions was for the kids." She shrugged. "Grown-ups don't need two pairs of hiking boots."

"What did you want to tell me last night?" I asked her.

"Let's talk about it later," she said, looking down and walking faster.

"*Now,* please," I begged. My knees turned to Silly Putty, because I could tell she had something to hide, something she didn't want to say.

"After breakfast?" she asked.

"Now!"

Instead of walking into the mess hall, we turned down the road toward the lake.

"Well," she began, glancing back to see if anybody was following us, "last night when everybody *seemed* settled, around ten o'clock if you can believe that, I went down and made a telephone call to . . . to a friend. When nobody answered, I got to thinking about meeting you at the phone the night before and how homesick you seemed, and I thought maybe it would help . . ." She took a deep breath before going on. ". . . maybe it might help if I brought you a big hello from your folks and good news from home, since you couldn't call yourself, and—"

"You're kidding. So you *called* them?"

She put her finger to her mouth to quiet me. There were only a dozen or so kids left to go in to breakfast, so she started talking fast.

"I wanted to help." She wiped her palms on her painters' pants and went on. "I've taken lots of psychology courses in school. I don't know why I thought a marshmallow could be the answer."

"What did they say? Were they home?" I didn't see how marshmallows had anything to do with it.

"I spoke to your mother."

"What did she *say?*"

"Well, everything is all right," she began, putting her hand on my arm, "but it isn't. I just don't want you to worry. Your mother doesn't want you to worry. It's not what you think."

"It's not what *I* think. It's what everybody *says*."

"Whatever. Your mother was right by the phone when I called. She said she was thinking about calling you, but was afraid it was too late."

"Too *late?*"

"At night."

I sank down on the cold concrete bench overlooking the lake. The skunk smell was almost gone.

"She was going to tell you," Miss Ivanovitch

said, sitting beside me, "that your father is in the hospital. He had gallstones."

"Hospital? Gallstones? I never heard of gallstones."

"It's, well, the gallbladder is a little sack that holds fluid from your liver and sometimes—mostly in very heavy people—it gets stones in it and sometimes the stones cause it to hurt."

"My dad is pretty fat, but where would he get a bag of stones?" I asked her. This is a phony story, I thought. I never heard such a phony story. "My dad has gas a lot," I said.

I guess she could tell I didn't believe her. "The stones *form* in the bag," she went on, leaning forward, serious, like I *had* to believe her. "It hurt so much, Hobie, they took his gallbladder out."

"Took it out?"

"Operated. They were at the hospital night before last when you called. She was even going to drive up for you, but she didn't want to leave him, and besides, the hospital doesn't allow ten-year-olds to visit." She sighed. "I stopped by last night to talk to you about it and kind of prepare you for today like your mom asked me to. But I thought, later, that the skunk attack was enough excitement for one night."

"Wait a minute," I said, "what does all this have to do with a divorce?"

She looked up, startled. Mr. Star was heading

down the path toward us. "Nobody knows I called," she said. "Listen, it was probably the wrong thing for me to do. Certainly it was against the rules."

"Divorce?" I asked again.

She shook her head. "Your mother thought that was a crazy idea. She said she guessed you really were homesick."

"But it wasn't crazy. Everybody . . ." I could feel my face turn red as I realized what it was. It was Telephone. It was Camp Trotter-Damp Daughter. It was Mrs. Bosco's voice shouting across the gym and the ladies at the booth where I bought chances. Lisa hadn't known anything after all.

". . . a lot of pain," she was saying, "but your mom said he's smiling again. It'll be OK. She said to tell you."

Mr. Star reached us, his whole face a question. "Can I help?" he asked.

My stomach was churning. Miss Ivanovitch looked at me and I shook my head at her.

"No, it was just . . ." she said.

"I had a . . ." we both started talking at once. Mr. Star waited, but neither of us went on.

"There might not be any scrambled eggs left if we stay out here much longer," he said.

I ran ahead, wondering how much she'd tell him. For two nights and almost three days I'd worried about phony things. And now I was so glad my parents weren't divorced I wasn't even scared about real stones in a sack. The woolly-worms were gone.

After cold scrambled eggs, we packed our bags and stripped our beds. Miss Ivanovitch gathered us around for our last Outdoor Education project. The Scotch Tape was scheduled for orienteering. That meant we were supposed to find our way with compasses. Only we didn't stick together. After Miss Ivanovitch talked about poles and paces for a while, she split us up into twos. Marshall and I were a team. She gave us paper with stuff written on it like "Go NNE 5 paces. Go S 9 paces," so that at the end you'd expect to dig for Bluebeard's treasure chest and giants' bones. My pace wasn't the same as Marshall's, but at last we found our gold treasure anyway, hanging from a tree branch—two bananas in a brown bag.

Wolfing them down, we made our way back to the clearing that was the meeting place for our group. Molly and Lisa were there playing catch with Miss Ivanovitch's hiking boot. They hadn't gotten a list of SSW and NE 13 paces stuff like we had. Instead, their paper had told them to find the boot, and fast. And they had. But they were tossing it so high, it was going to end up as a bird nest if they weren't careful.

Miss Ivanovitch was off orienteering with Vince because there were an uneven number of kids in my group. I hoped their path wasn't covered with thorns or broken beer bottles, because those yellow-and-white stripes weren't going to keep out much.

"Look what *I* found," Molly called, tossing the shoe at Lisa with one hand and holding up a piece of paper with the other.

"It's a rubbing. We found it in a bush, like it was growing there," Lisa said, grabbing the pitch. "There must have been a cyclone last night to drag it so far from the graveyard."

"I didn't hear a wind," Molly said.

"There was a lot of action," I told them, "after midnight."

"And I suppose *you* were out after midnight?" Molly laughed.

"Can I see the paper?" I asked her, knowing what it was.

"*I* found it," Molly said, holding it behind her.

"But it's mine," I told her.

"Prove it."

"It's a purple cupid with a moustache."

She turned around, peeked inside the rolled-up paper, and then looked back at me, very suspicious.

"How did you know?"

I shrugged. "I know because it's mine."

"But it *rained* the night we were at the graveyard, and this rubbing hasn't been rained on. A car's run over it, though." She flipped it past me so I could see the tracks on one corner.

"If you'd asked me about the tracks, I could have told you about them, too," I lied. I almost snatched it, but Nick would have killed me if I'd torn that one too.

Lisa leaned over and fingered the tire tracks on the paper. "You sure don't take good care of your stuff to have it, like, floating around under cars."

"OK," Molly demanded, "explain about why it didn't get wet."

"You wouldn't believe me."

"You're right."

Miss Ivanovitch came jogging up with Vince, a bag of banana peels in her hand. ". . . climbed sheer cliffs when I was on Outward Bound," she was telling him. And then she saw the rubbing of the angel.

"Oh, Molly, you have my picture! Wherever did you find it?" She held out her hand.

Molly put the rubbing behind her back again and stepped away. "Hobie said it was *his*. He described it. Can you?"

Miss Ivanovitch looked flustered. "But it's . . ."

Nick and Aretha ran up behind Molly and Lisa, the fourth pair back.

"Molly," Nick yelled, spotting the angel. "I take back everything gross I ever said about you. You've found my rubbing. I thought it was gone for good."

"*Your* rubbing?" She held it out at arm's length and stared. "What's so incredibly cueshee about

136

this, anyway? Mine was much better. This angel has a moustache.''

"Oh, does it?" Miss Ivanovitch cried. "That's fantastic." Suddenly, she raised her chin up high, held out both hands, and said, "Molly Bosco, I'd like two things, and I'd like them promptly. First, I'll take my shoe, and," she smiled at Nick and me, "and then I'll have *my* rubbing."

Molly blinked, looked at us to see if we'd complain and, when we didn't, handed them over. Then she turned away and, shrugging like she couldn't care less, pulled Lisa down on the ground with her. They started balancing acorn caps on twigs.

Miss Ivanovitch handed us the rubbing. "Sign it in small letters—both of you—down by the tire track," she said, taking a red pen from her big bag and handing it over. "Not that I'm likely to forget. It's just that I'm framing it to hang in a special place, so it ought to be signed."

I could imagine our rubbing right over a fireplace with candles burning on each side. And I could see her and Mr. Star standing in front, smiling up at it.

"You gonna put your boot on now?" Nick asked her.

"Maybe not," she told him, tilting her head. "I'm just getting used to walking askew."

"What I want to know," Molly said, "is *when* you guys did that rubbing, whichever of you did do it." She flung an acorn top, like a frog's

Frisbee. "I've been thinking, and I don't know when it could have been. There just wasn't any time."

"Some things are mysteries that will never be solved, Molly," Miss Ivanovitch told her, and she hurried off to greet two more banana eaters.

For lunch I was hopper again for hot dogs and potato chips. Then we played one last kickball game up on the high field, the smell of skunk still faint in the air. The story was, Mr. Star told us, that a farmer's dog had tangled with a skunk and lost. I was glad we hadn't barked at Kitty-Kitty.

The score was four-all when Eugene shouted, "The buses, they're here!" He hadn't had his eyes off the road for the whole game. The buses were pure sunshine. I had never noticed before that they smile. These were grinning from fender to fender.

After I tossed my little red suitcase up to the driver, who was packing them in the bus, I looked back one last time at Camp Damp Daughter lodge. Somebody had hung his underwear on the sign.

I settled down in a window seat. The heater was on, so it felt steamy, like August.

"Whad's dad smell?" Nick asked, holding his nose and looking at me. I smelled it, too. It was near. People were staring. The heat made it stronger. Nick broke up and dug a rose-perfume-drenched Kleenex from my pocket and tossed it toward the back of the bus. It smelled like predator-prey. And it smelled like Mrs. Bosco, too.

"Better than skunk," he said, laughing. I poked him in the ribs, but it isn't at all bad, the smell of roses. As the bus moved, my head felt heavy and my eyes kept flapping shut. Whenever I thought of the gallstones I remembered Miss Ivanovitch saying, "It'll be OK," and the gallstones would disappear and turn to granite or marble or skipping stones across the lake. I slept.

The bus was rumbling up Central Street toward school when I woke. Nick was shaking my shoulder.

"Except for the green slime mountain," Nick said, "and the wrecked semi that spilled three hundred porcupines on the highway, and Eugene getting sick again in the back of the bus, you didn't miss a thing." I opened my eyes as wide as I could. He shook me again. "And if you don't wake up they leave you on and you go back for three more days of peanut butter and jelly stew."

"Three days!" I shook my head. It seemed a whole lot more like three weeks we'd been gone.

"We played Animal, Vegetable, and Mineral while you were zonked out," Molly said, turning around in her seat.

"Yeah," Nick moaned. "We played it a lot. One time you were the answer. You were vegetable."

"Nick!" Lisa yelped. "That's, like, not true. I *never* called Hobie a vegetable."

"Maybe not," Nick said, shrugging, "but you *laughed* when we said 'animal.' "

I rubbed my eyes and focused on the group waiting on the sidewalk, peering at the buses. Mrs. Ezry was there, aiming her camera, waiting for the After shot. My mother was at work. Or at the hospital. Mrs. Rossi was going to pick Nick and me up, but she wasn't around either.

Miss Hutter and Mrs. Bosco were already waiting on the steps of the school. Either our buses were slow or Mrs. Bosco had been hot-dogging it down the highway in her Honda trying to beat us back.

As we climbed off the bus, Mrs. Bosco stepped forward and boomed, "Welcome home. Welcome home after your wonderful adventure." And when Miss Ivanovitch stepped off, she said, "Boys and girls, there's going to be an announcement. I'm sure there is. Miss Ivanovitch has something to tell you all." She beamed.

Miss Ivanovitch blushed. She stuck her hands in her pockets. "I'm not sure. What if something . . ." Mr. Star grinned at her.

"Go ahead, Svetlana. Tell them. They'll be tickled," he said.

Molly tightened her lips and crossed her arms to keep the news out.

Behind us two mountains of bags were rising on the sidewalk where the drivers were tossing them. Some kids were rushing off to get theirs, in a hurry to get home. Most of 4B stood, though, with our mouths open, waiting, when a green van tooled up in front of the buses and a red-haired man in a black-and-white check jacket bounded out. He hurried over to where we were standing like he was late, and I wondered whose father he was. I'd never seen him before. As he walked he smiled at the ground instead of us, but when he looked up, it was straight at Miss Ivanovitch.

She grabbed his hand and pulled him forward. "I'd like you to meet my friends," she told him. He was only a couple of inches taller than she was, but big. He was big like he lifted weights, not like he ate too much chocolate chip cheesecake like my dad.

"This is Miss Hutter, the principal; Mrs. Bosco; Jack Star; and these," she said, nodding at the group of us stacked up near the door of the bus, "these are a fraction of the 4B's." He shook hands with us all. "This is Edward Kinsella," she told us, like that explained everything.

When Edward Kinsella finished shaking everybody's hands, he took hers. And he held it. We stared, just as we had at her hand and Mr. Star's in the campfire circle.

"Is he your brother?" Aretha asked. Mr. Kinsella grinned.

Miss Ivanovitch took her hand away and reached for her green duffle just tossed on the stack.

"Are you a teacher?" Michelle asked Edward Kinsella.

"Animal, vegetable, or mineral?" I asked him.

He laughed. "I'm a telephone lineman. When the phones stop, I set them right."

"I was looking for him to say goodbye to us when we left for camp," Miss Ivanovitch told us, lugging the duffle back to the group.

"An emergency," he apologized to her. "Some cable-TV guys sheared one of our lines. And a lot of wires were down night before last. Did it storm up by you?"

"Oh, yes," we said.

"Oh, wow."

"Lightning in the dark with sparks and ghosts."

"And a tree down by the lake."

"Oh, yes," we said.

"Is that," I asked her, "who you tried to call?"

"Right," she laughed. "He wasn't home either."

We followed along as she tossed her duffle into the back of the van. I hoped the landing didn't smash the angel.

Molly stepped forward and said, "What's this big announcement about you and Mr. Star?"

Miss Ivanovitch threw back her head and laughed. "Molly, my dear, I think you were the only girl in 4B who wasn't trying to play matchmaker with me and Mr. Star."

Molly frowned. That was no answer.

"But," Lisa asked, "but which one are you going to marry?"

Miss Ivanovitch eyed us all and shook her head. "Ah," she said, "while I do hate to disappoint you, I don't have plans to marry anybody."

I think Mr. Star smiled. He must have been worried, too.

Molly looked suspicious.

"Something you should know," Mr. Star said to us, filling in the silence, "is that fourth grade and fifth are going to be in the same hall next year. We're moving things around this summer."

"And I'm going to hang one of your gravestone rubbings in the new hall," Miss Ivanovitch said, nodding to Nick and me.

"You're hanging it?" Molly asked. "Why you?"

"Me," Miss Ivanovitch answered, "because Miss Hutter has asked me to come to Central School next year to teach fifth grade." She looked around proudly. "Mr. Swansong is moving to Iceland. I'll be taking his place in 5B."

"Smile!" Mrs. Ezry called, kneeling down in the grass and aiming up at us. We smiled automatically, even Molly, while the programs in our heads got rewritten.

"You," Eugene said slowly, "are going to teach fifth grade at our school next year?"

"Yes," she told him, "my very first year as a regular teacher."

"That's really wonderful," he told her, and he

143

shook her hand before heading off to where his mother stood waiting. She'd been waving to him and calling something in a language I didn't understand.

"Then," I said, suddenly realizing it, "we might get you next year."

"There are two teachers, so it's a fifty-fifty chance." She hopped into the van, rolled down the window, and called, "Keep clear of crocodiles and creatures of the night." She waved at us with both hands as they drove away.

"Isn't that lovely," Mrs. Bosco said. She tugged at her cowboy kerchief. "Don't you think it's absolutely lovely, Molly?"

"I don't believe it. I don't believe Miss Hutter would do that to us," Molly said, dragging her suitcase behind her.

"It's terrific," Aretha yelled, and ran to claim her bag.

"Smile," Mrs. Ezry called again, and those of us who were still left smiled.

"Hobart," Miss Hutter said, drawing me aside, "about our lunch at the Chuckwagon tomorrow."

"Oh, lunch," I told her, "I meant to tell you about lunch . . ." I'd totally forgotten to make up a foolproof excuse short of pneumonia. I wiggled my tooth with my tongue, but it hung in there. Too bad. It would have bled like crazy.

"Come to my office directly after the lunch bell—"

"No kidding, that's all right. I can just eat at

144

school. They're having tuna casserole in the cafeteria tomorrow anyway, and that's my favorite.''

Rolf stepped right up to see me suffer. He was swinging his sack of Articles To Be Left at Home, and he had a smirk as wide as a smiley face. When Miss Hutter glanced at him, he was grinning so big, she smiled back.

"I have an idea," she said. "Why don't you bring one of your friends along . . ."

"But I—"

"Perhaps Rolf would like to join us." She looked at him with interest.

"Sure, Rolf," I said, whomping him on the back. "Miss Hutter and I would like you to have a hamburger with us at the Chuckwagon tomorrow. Got any other plans for noon? No, of course you don't. Noon is lunchtime. That's great."

"I . . . I . . ." he gagged.

"He'd love to," I told her. "He's just naturally shy. Thanks, Miss Hutter."

As she hurried off to the office, I told him, "It'll be a ball, Rolf, no kidding. We'll tell her all about trucking. And the next time you're in the office for skateboarding in the cafeteria, you'll have something to talk about."

Brong, bronk. We jumped at the horn. Mrs. Rossi and Toby pulled up in their little gray station wagon. "Sorry to be late," she called as she climbed out, but—"

I hurried over. "How is Dad?" I asked.

"You already know?" She sighed. "Oh, good.

145

I'd been worrying about how to explain gallstones. The dictionary didn't help." She leaned over till she was exactly my height and said, "Hobie, he spent much too long pretending it didn't hurt, but he's OK. The doctor tells him he has to lose some weight, and your mother says he'll hate that." She hurried over to hug Nick. He hugged her back like he'd missed her too.

Toby, his dinosaur cape on wrong-side out, bounced, *kapong,* out of the car. "Ribbit-roogie," he said.

"Hi, Tobe, who are you?" I asked him.

"Ribbit-roogie," he croaked again, springing forward on his toes.

"He's a frogosaurus," his mother laughed, "and he's been very jumpy waiting for you guys to come home."

"Did you put the fish to bed? Were there tarantulas?" Toby asked Nick as he hurried to the car. "Was there a lion?"

"There was a cat who thought he was an owl, and there was a skunk called Kitty-Kitty," Nick told him, and Toby laughed. He knew a good lie when he heard one.

"What did you do?" Toby asked me, grabbing me by the leg and digging his heels into the ground.

What I did, I thought, was make it through two nights with nobody but Miss Ivanovitch and the woollyworms knowing how bad I wanted to be home.

"Talk to me!" Toby said. "What was it *like?*"

I leaned over, opened the car door, and tossed my red bag inside. "It was wild," I told him, poking him in his soft frogosaurus belly. "It was wild."

ABOUT THE AUTHOR

JAMIE GILSON was born in Beardstown, Illinois. She graduated from Northwestern University with a B.S. degree in radio/television education. Ms. Gilson is a former junior high school teacher and radio, television and film writer/ producer. In addition to writing books, she now writes for *Chicago* magazine, lectures, and holds writing and poetry workshops in the Chicago area.

Jamie Gilson's *Thirteen Ways to Sink a Sub,* which was honored as an A.L.A. *Booklist* Children's Reviewer's Choice, is also about the kids in class 4B. Her other titles available as Archway Paperbacks include *Do Bananas Chew Gum?,* which won the 1982 Carl Sandburg Award and the Charlie May Simon Children's Book Award in Arkansas; *Dial Leroi Rupert, DJ*; and *Can't Catch Me, I'm the Gingerbread Man*.

Ms. Gilson and her husband Jerome, a trademark lawyer, have three children, Tom, Matthew and Anne. They live in Wilmette, Illinois, a suburb of Chicago.